Solomon Isaiah Spreewell

Throw-Up, Pigs & Kisses

By

Shannon Gepford

SC AV

Phil 4:13

ISBN: 1-4033-1454-3 (e-book)
ISBN: 1-4033-1455-1 (Paperback)
ISBN: 1-4033-3212-6 (Hardcover)

Library of Congress Control Number 2002091066

This book is printed on acid free paper.

Printed in the United States of America
Bloomington, IN

1stBooks — rev. 09/06/02

Thank you and Dedication page:

If it wasn't for the generous help and encouragement from the following people, this book may have never made it into print:

- My sister, Karmin Ricker, English Teacher at Drexel High School in Drexel, Missouri, for helping me proofread and reminding me that some of the incidents in this book that paralleled our lives were not ingrained in her memory the same way they were in mine.

- Sheila Adkins, English Teacher at Adrian High School in Adrian, Missouri, for helping me proofread and encouraging me not to give up and to go ahead and finish this book even when I was doubtful.

- Vicki Moser, English Teacher at Adrian Jr. High School in Adrian, Missouri, for helping me proofread and for giving me a good basis of which to write, thanks to my year in her sixth grade class.

- Rebecca Palmer, Gifted Education Teacher at Pleasant Hill Elementary School in Pleasant Hill, Missouri, for reading this book to her class as a test audience while it was still in manuscript form.

- Annie Curry, a special friend of mine who was the first person to read the finished manuscript and convince her teacher, Mrs. Palmer to read it to her class.

- Our Heavenly Father for blessing me with the ability to write and use humor as a basis to tell a story. All my gifts come from God and for that I am truly thankful. **Phillipians 4:13** (NIV) states *"I can do everything through him who gives me strength."*

iii

Table of Contents

1.   My Nickname-Sis.. 1

2.   Spreewell County Stadium............................. 32

3.   Pig Pond... 56

4.   Our Sentence... 83

5.   Chris Scofield & Lunch Room Cockroach.... 93

6.   "Going with"…... 109

7.   Kisses.. 124

8.   What is the Capitol of Missouri?.................. 136

9.   Go'un to the Game?... 146

10.   Bleacher Jumpin'... 154

Chapter 1

My Nickname-Sis

Hello, my name is Solomon Isaiah Spreewell. My friends, enemies, Mom, Dad, and basically anyone that has even vaguely heard of me call me by my nickname-Sis. What a nickname it proves to be. My parents must have not been thinking when they coined my birth name. I can understand the reason behind why they chose Solomon. They hoped that I would turn out to be this awesome type of person that would be very wise. They must have figured that since the biblical Solomon was the smartest man in the Bible, and because he was such a great ruler, if I shared his name just maybe some of his special "powers" would

1

be granted to me by the grace of God. Unfortunately, I have no clue why they chose Isaiah as my middle name, except for the fact that my parents are deeply religious and that Isaiah was an Old Testament prophet.

If my parents would have been thinking, they would have known that such an outdated name would be the butt of many jokes and the target of years of ridicule. But they weren't, so I was stuck with an outlandish name that I couldn't spell for most of my primary years. Luckily, my classmates were not going to be nuclear physicists because over half of them couldn't spell their own names until they were in middle school, so at least they couldn't make fun of me for being an inadequate speller.

Since we as a group had trouble putting letters of the alphabet together to form things that resembled words, we started neglecting to call each other by our real names. Instead, we picked out or made up nicknames for each other. For example, Catherine Hellwig was forever known as Cat, while Nicholas Gutterman earned the new name of D.B. because of his infatuation with diamondback rattlesnakes-weird! My nickname was simply picked from the first letters of my entire name. Whatever person thought that up was truly brilliant. You would think that surely someone would have been able to come up with a clever nickname for me like Heather Gordon did for Oscar Finch. After a series of visits to Mr. Bullock's office, Heather rephrased Oscar's name into Hall for his many trips down the long corridor.

3

Shannon Gepford

I have to admit, I didn't like my nickname very well, but it beat some of the other names that I was called or had been stuck with during my younger years. The one I hated the most was spawned by the brainchild himself, Carlos Muchado.

Carlos was an interesting person. He seemed to always be doing something that he wasn't supposed to. I swear that he did stupid things just to make people hate him even more than they did the day before. If the class had a bully, I guess Carlos qualified even though no one was scared of him. The class as a whole kind of dismissed him as being an ignorant, pathetic slob of a human with no idea of how well he was actually disliked by the rest of the planet.

Carlos dressed himself-that is one thing I know for sure. The reason for my accurate assessment is based on the fact that if he was dressed by someone with even the slightest amount of taste, he would not have worn that ridiculous looking belt buckle that covered over half of his lower abdomen. He was so in love with his silver-plated, tarnished-from-wear medallion that he even wore it on Track & Field Day along with his bright orange tank top and pea green shorts. Funny thing though, I never did figure out how that obnoxious belt buckle stayed on since his shorts didn't have any belt loops, and Carlos wasn't wearing a belt! It's a good thing that the fashion police were in another sector of the school that day, or Carlos would surely have been fined.

I remember the day that I earned a spin-off nickname from Carlos. It seemed like it happened just yesterday, partly because Carlos reminds me of when, where, why, and how he tagged me with it, partly because I don't want to be associated with it, and partly because the very thought of it makes me cringe.

The day that I was to receive royal humiliation started out just like a normal day in the fifth grade. I awoke just a little after six o'clock. I did my typical morning routine: Beat my sister Andie to the bathroom. Sauntered down the stairs into the living room. Set the thirty-minute timer above the piano. Played Mozart, Bach, and Spreewell (my own select compositions) until I had used up the thirty minutes. Sprung into the romper room to pump some serious iron (to keep me stronger than "bullies" like Carlos). Gobbled down two bowls of *Captain Crunch Cereal.* Brushed my teeth. Rounded up Andie. Walked a quarter of a mile to get on the bus. Then rode to school.

Once at school, everything seemed to be fine until the 8:30 bell rang for class to start. At that moment the class let out a collective groan as Mr. Bullock walked into the classroom. Being perceptive, we all realized that our normal fifth grade teacher was "not among the living" (a term used for anyone who was absent on a particular day).

Mr. Bullock proceeded to tell us that Mrs. Sauerborn had contracted a virus and would be gone for a couple of days. He also informed us that he was going to be the substitute while she was gone. These tidbits of information led to an array of questions that Mr. Bullock fielded about as well as a shortstop without a glove.

"What is a virus?" yelled Gretchen.

"It's something that causes people to get sick," replied Mr. Bullock.

"Can animals get sick from it?" crooned Billy.

"Yes, I'm sure that they can," responded Mr. Bullock.

"Will Mrs. Sauerborn's cat get sick too?" questioned Sadie.

"Who cares about her stupid fur-ball of a cat?" screamed Carlos, "That dumb thing scratched me the last time I tried to pet it."

"That's just because you picked it up by the tail," interjected Sadie almost crying.

Carlos started to return the answer, "That's what tails..." when Mr. Bullock interrupted with his principal type-voice "Enough is enough. If you have a question, raise your hand one at a time and I will do my best to answer it."

The first person to raise his hand was Roger Twiddle a.k.a. Twid. Twid was extremely fast. He could outrun everyone in the fifth grade, and he thought he could beat the sixth graders also. He claimed that the "sixth graders were afraid to race him because it would be too embarrassing to lose to a fifth grader."

The whole time the class was bombarding Mr. Bullock with questions, Roger was sizing up the situation at hand. He inquisitively asked, "Mr. Bullock, if you're not in your office because you're subbing, who will take care of the rest of the school if it has problems, or if someone gets in trouble who will punish them?" After a moment of silence, Mr. Bullock replied with as much wisdom as he could muster in such a short period of time, "My secretary, Mrs. White, will handle any problems that come up. But I really doubt that there will be any trouble today."

That answer seemed to satisfy almost everyone in the room except Roger. He suddenly got this weird look on his face but remained silent. Mr. Bullock gazed around the room with a feeling of content as no one raised their hand for any further questions. Even though Roger had kept his hand still, I could tell that his mind was racing.

I had been Roger's best friend for about three years. Because of our close friendship, I could easily tell when Roger was not satisfied with an answer, and this was one of those times. If you know Roger as well as I do, you realize two things about him. First, his mind is constantly moving light speeds ahead of everyone else which causes his eyebrows to wrinkle just above his nose and his nostrils to flare. This is a dead give away that he is calculating something mischievous. Secondly, his curiosity often gets him into trouble, but his charming good looks and loveable personality usually get him off the hook. As I said earlier, I realized that Roger was thinking about something, and I couldn't wait until recess to find out just what it was.

After the initial shock to the classroom, the class settled down and adjusted to Mr. Bullock.

He took roll, noted that there were no absences, and then told us to get out our spelling books. Spelling went by without a hitch, so we were on our way to start social studies when Mr. Bullock announced, "Let's take a break. Roger, Sis, I mean-Solomon, and Frank may use the boy's restroom while Catherine, Sadie, and Chris may use the girl's."

I thought that this was peculiar since we didn't normally take a break until after recess at about 10:20 a.m., but I really didn't mind. There was no way that I was going to turn down a chance to relax even if I didn't have to use the restroom. Besides, now I could find out what was on Roger's mind about an hour before I had planned.

When we entered the restroom, Roger still had his wrinkled, eyebrow-flared nose look so I proceeded to whisper, "Whatcha thinkun?"

"Shhhhh!" Roger replied, "I don't want Frank to hear."

We waited until Frank had washed his hands and started heading out of the restroom before we started talking again.

"What's going on?" I quizzed.

"D.B. brought some chew! I saw him take it out of his coat pocket and give Oscar and Carlos a can each this morning. I think it was *Skoal*," said Roger.

My mind was on fire. I knew that I couldn't tell Mr. Bullock about the situation, but I also knew right from wrong. I finally decided just to play it off because just maybe it wasn't actually tobacco inside those cans. Maybe it was dried beef jerky. Yeah, that was a possibility; Oscar's dad had just killed an eight point buck. We left the restroom and headed back to class.

Upon our return, we found the class busy reading their social studies book. Each of us sat down and started reading about the *Mayflower,* Plymouth Rock, and the first Thanksgiving. Mrs. Sauerborn's instructions were for us to read through this text and answer the questions at the end of the chapter before we went to recess. Mr. Bullock followed them to perfection since he wouldn't let Angela go to recess until she was finished with her work.

Finally, we were outside the walls of the school. We all raced to the football field in hopes of being the first class there. To our dismay, the sixth graders had already beaten us to the field; therefore, we had to find something else to occupy our recess time since there wasn't enough room for both grades to play. Most of the girls and a few of the boys played near the swings as they attempted to play a sport that used a black and white checkered ball that you couldn't touch with your hands unless you were guarding a net. Furthermore, this sport wasn't even invented in America. It was called soccer, and it was invented in Scotland or somewhere else across the Atlantic Ocean. Our group of guys had decided earlier that since we should "buy American," we should surely play only American sports; and if we couldn't play football during football season, then we would find something else to do. I do believe, however, that we would have let down our macho American image if we had known the rules to this foreign game because it had to be better than standing around watching everyone else.

"Hey, let's play Red Rover behind the football tower," stated D.B.

"Yeah," we all responded in unison.

"It sure beats standing around watchun' the girls play soccer," interjected Oscar as he bowed and held his hands to his side as if he were doing a curtsy.

Within ten seconds, we were all behind the tower getting ready to choose sides. It was Carlos's and Pat's turn to be captain. Carlos started the event by choosing D. B. Pat then chose Roger.

Carlos screamed, "You jug-head! I wanted Twid."

"Too bad," volleyed Pat, "you should have picked him first."

Carlos then chose Oscar while Pat chose me. In the end, each team had five players. Carlos finished out with Sam and Joe while Pat finished with Louis and Frank.

"Before we start kicking your backside, we're gonna take a dip," announced D. B.

"Hey, any of you losers want a dip?" questioned Oscar.

"You can't do that at school!" jolted Frank.

"Sure we can. Mrs. Sauerborn isn't here, and Mr. Bullock has no idea that we brought it to school. Besides he's too busy watchun' the girly-men play soccer," retorted D. B. as he popped open his can of *Skoal.*

This action seemed to be all the permission needed for the rest of the henchmen to get their cans out of their pockets and pack it with their index finger before opening their cans. I had always thought that it was really neat the way a person could make his index finger loose enough so that when you shook your wrist you could make a popping sound on the outside of the can, while you were packing the dip on the inside into a clump. Even in that moment, I had the slightest bit of admiration for these rebels-partly because they could make the popping sound that I couldn't and partly because they were either brave enough or stupid enough to try something this foolish and think they could get away with it. I guessed this was what "living on the edge" was all about.

"Want some?" Oscar drooled as he held out his can to Sam.

"Oh, I don't think..." started Sam as he was interrupted by Carlos who thundered, "Don't be a mega-weinie like the girly-men who play soccer. Be a man and take some."

At that point, Sam reached over and scooped up a clump of the nasty looking brown stuff that had a wintergreen scent to it. He carefully positioned it between his thumb and his index finger and gingerly lodged it between his cheek and his lower molars on the right side of his mouth. This seemed to be all the prodding that Joe and Pat needed as each of them took a dip from Oscar's can. Now, everyone had a dip except Roger, Louis, Frank, and me.

"You women gonna take a hit?" chortled Carlos.

I responded with a very emphatic, "No, that stuff will kill you!"

"You just won't admit it, but you're a sissy, Sis. You're afraid that you'll get caught and that will ruin your perfect image," challenged Carlos.

"That's not it you clueless wonder. I don't want to do something that will hurt my body," I proclaimed.

"Nice cover-up, Sis. You're just afraid that you'll get caught," quoted D. B.

"If I was afraid of that, I wouldn't be out here with you idiots!" I exclaimed.

"Face it, Sis. You're just a big sissy. If you're not, you'll prove it and take a dip; otherwise, you'll just be a big sissy, which by the way fits your nickname. Sis really stands for sister anyway doesn't it? Your parents wanted a girl so badly that they gave you a girl's nickname," rebounded Carlos. Everyone chuckled in delight. After his beautiful hammering of me, Carlos once again held out his hand indicating for me to take a dip, but once again I refused.

"Sissy, Sissy, Sissy," murmured Carlos as he spat a stream of brown liquid in my direction.

"If Sissy won't take some, then maybe you will," offered Oscar while he glared down his nose at Roger.

"Well...," stammered Twid as he shuffled his feet while trying to make up his mind, "I guess just a small dip wouldn't hurt."

At that moment I knew Roger was going to take the chance. His eyebrows were wrinkled and his nostrils were flared. Obviously, the whole time Carlos had been bombarding me with insults, Roger had been weighing his options. Somewhere in his mind, Roger was able to justify his action even though he knew what the consequences were if he were to get caught. I guess that this was the type of event that Roger needed on a regular basis to satisfy his appetite for adventure.

21

"Let's start the game before recess is over," pleaded Louis in a hoping tone. Louis figured that if we started playing then, maybe his manhood wouldn't be challenged since he didn't want a dip either. I have to admit that I was relieved that we were about to start because I had taken enough heckling for one recess.

Both teams clasped their hands in a straight line while facing each other about twenty yards apart. We were about to begin when Mr. Bullock walked up. "I hope you boys don't mind me watching you play," stated Mr. Bullock. "I can only handle watching so much soccer." At that point, you could have heard a pin drop.

Things do have a way of always working themselves out. Before Mr. Bullock arrived, the most prominent noises were the zip and splat sounds. The zip sound came from the mouths of the tobacco dippers as they let fly another wad of spit into the air. The splat sound was just the echo of the spit hitting the ground. Now, no one could let any more spit fly, or Mr. Bullock would know the crime.

Carlos's team started the game by shouting in garbled unison, "Red Rover, Red Rover, send Sissy right over." This meant that I had to run as fast as I could and try to break through the outstretched arms of the other team. I chose to try to break the bond between Sam and Joe. In the twenty yards between Sam and Joe's arms and myself, I was able to build up enough speed to cause their arms to part upon impact. Because of my prowess, I was able to return to my team and bring Sam and Joe with me. If I had not been successful, I would have had to stay on Carlos's team.

"How's that for a Sissy?" I questioned as I jogged back to my line.

D. B. hissed," Just wait until you call my name. I'll cut through that line just as a rattlesnake would devour a mouse."

Our group decided to call on Oscar. Our reasoning was simple. Oscar had a funny look on his face. His eyes were squinted and a white crust was forming on his lips. His face was even starting to turn a pale white. We knew something was wrong because he hadn't said anything since Mr. Bullock had showed up. "Red Rover, Red Rover, send Hall right over," we shouted.

Oscar started up his engine and ran with as much speed as he could muster. He had decided to break the bond between Roger and Pat. The closer he got to the line, the more distorted his face became. It appeared as if each step really pained him. He finally reached their arms and smashed into them with his belly. At that instant, he let out a tremendous groan. All three boys were sent flying backwards. Roger and Pat were sprawled flat on their backs while Oscar was stretched out across them. Amazingly, Roger and Pat still had their hands locked together.

Each boy picked himself up off the ground and dusted the grass away from his clothes. Oscar still had the pale white look on his face, but it seemed to be spreading to other parts of his body. Suddenly, Oscar grabbed his stomach and started to run to the other side of the tower. Unfortunately, he only got about three steps when he suddenly had to stop and bend over to relieve some of the pressure in his stomach. As he was bent over, he creaked out the words, "I think I'm gonna hurl!" Within two seconds his mouth opened wide, and his eyes started to bug out. His body lurched forward as his feet gave in causing him to fall to his knees. He quickly placed his hands on the ground to give his body balance since his head was already swimming in a sea of stars. The next thing to happen was one of the most unpleasant sights that I had seen in my eleven years. Out of his mouth spewed something that resembled molten lava forced from a volcano. It was brownish-red with small white chunks in it, and it covered about a three-foot area. It also gave off a dreadfully foul stench that surely helped to kill the grass in that area.

"He must have had oatmeal for breakfast," giggled Louis.

Frank and I quietly reasoned between us that since Mr. Bullock arrived, Oscar hadn't been able to spit and that he was swallowing the tobacco juice, which caused his stomach to boil. "I guess that the crash Oscar had between Pat and Roger sent his stomach over the edge," I whispered.

"Yeah, what a momma's boy! Just guess he couldn't handle the stuff," mimicked Frank.

"How, nasty!" screamed Louis. At that point Frank and I turned around in time to see Roger and Pat start into gagging convulsions. We knew what was going to happen next. Both boys suddenly assumed the launching position as did Oscar just a few seconds earlier. The next detail was tremendous. Mr. Bullock had walked over to see if the boys were okay and upon arriving at the scene, he realized that they were also

27

about to "lose their lunch." Quickly sidestepping, Mr. Bullock swerved out of the way of the projectile vomit launched in his direction by Roger. To his dismay, he stepped right in the way of Pat's stream. Mr. Bullock's whole left side was covered with a brownish liquid.

"If I didn't know any better, I'd have to say that Pat didn't eat any breakfast since there aren't any visible chunks," mused Louis.

"Looks like he had tea for breakfast," added Frank.

Mr. Bullock started shaking his left hand as some of the left over spew dripped onto his fingers. He had a "why me" look on his face that seemed to say "Can this get any worse?"

Unfortunately, for him it did. When he shook his left hand, part of the vomit flew behind him where

Carlos was standing. The brown nasty slime nailed Carlos right in the mouth, which had been open wide, out of amazement. Almost upon impact, Carlos doubled over and joined in the party. This must have been all that the rest of the tobacco chewing group could handle as each one of them "joined in at the chorus" of gagging sounds and demonic noises that were gurgled from the pits of their stomachs.

After each of the boys' stomachs was purged, all of them lined up to go in from recess. The boys' were a truly pitiful sight. Their eyes had turned glassy while their faces were washed in a blank white stare. Each of them had the look of not being there as their mind drifted to a far away place. All of them had a definite stench engulfing their bodies, which made the rest of us in line stay at least twenty feet in front or behind them.

"Wasn't that cool!" chirped Louis.

"I don't know if cool is the appropriate word," I said.

"Serves 'em right," chimed in Frank.

"My sentiments exactly," I snickered as I made a point to give Carlos a glare. I hoped that because of the incident, Carlos would quit calling me Sissy. This later proved not to be the case. Just like any lowlife slug, he would manage to bring it up at the most inopportune times, if not for any other reason than just to make me mad because he knew that it touched a nerve inside me that I couldn't tolerate.

Once we returned to class, Mr. Bullock excused himself to go change. Mrs. White took over the classroom in his absence. She sent all of the "throw

up-group" to the nurse one at a time so they could

drink some *Pepto-Bismal* and *7Up* to calm their

stomachs. I don't think that it helped very much, as

none of the boys regained their original color until the

next day. Finally, Mr. Bullock returned wearing a

sweatsuit. He must have borrowed it from someone in

the P.E. department. The rest of the day went by as

smoothly as possible considering the morning's

adventures.

Chapter 2

Spreewell County Stadium

Over Christmas break during kindergarten, my family moved from the city limits of Wrigley, Missouri, to a farm about four and a half miles southeast of Wrigley. It was quite a shock to my system. Gone were the houses that sheltered some of my best friends within shouting distance. Gone were the constant noises of cars and trucks driving past my home at all hours of the day and night. Gone were the two block walks to Main Street where most of the businesses resided. Gone was the most important thing to me in my life—other kids to play games with.

It didn't matter to me what type of game it was. As long as it had a winner and a loser and involved some type of action, I was always ready to join in. I have to admit, I was a little partial to baseball and basketball, but that didn't stop me from playing other sports like football even though I wasn't really fond of the contact.

After only one day on the farm, I realized that if I wanted to continue playing sports, I would have to do one of three things. I would have to make up imaginary games that only one person could play. Con my sister, Andie, into playing with me (which was almost as good of an idea as taking a piece of meat from a starving lion), or continually have one of my friends spend the night with me. The only problem with the third choice was that I knew my parents wouldn't go for that idea since I wasn't allowed to have friends stay with me on a school night. Therefore, idea number three was delegated to only Fridays and Saturdays. That meant that I would have to find something to help combat the anti-sports blues, even if I had to lower my standards and accept the fact that I might have to use my first two ideas.

"Get up! Geeeet up! Come on you loser, get out of bed," I screamed as I yanked the covers off Andie's bed. "It's a beautiful day, and you're slowing my progress to the Major Leagues. Isn't that an awful thought to harbor for the rest of your life? The only reason that Solomon Isaiah Spreewell didn't become a Major League All-Star center fielder was because his sister, Andie, wouldn't get out of bed to help him practice on the most beautiful morning of the entire

Christmas vacation. That one day of missed practice was possibly enough to keep him from representing the Kansas City Royals in the annual midsummer classic—The All-Star Game. I can hear..." I lobbied as my voice trailed off while I dodged pillows, stuffed animals, Barbie dolls, and hair barrettes that Andie was flinging at me in an effort to drive me from her room. When I finally crossed the threshold to the hall on the way out of her room, a loud crack rang in my ears as Andie slammed her door almost catching my blessed right arm in its wake. Remembering that I hadn't finished my last statement, which was an effort to make her feel guilty, I concluded. "I can still hear Mel Allen and Vin Scully (my two favorite baseball announcers) telling my life story, and the only reason that I wasn't starting in the All-Star game was because

35

of that one day of missed practice thanks to my sister, Andie. By the way, nice arm, but you need the practice too. Obviously, we need to work on your accuracy, or you would have hit me with one of those flying objects. Get dressed and meet me outside in ten minutes!" I screamed through the closed, solid-wood door.

"Oh shut up! I'll be there when I get there and not a second before," roared Andie from behind the door.

"Don't worry, another couple of minutes of beauty sleep won't help you. When things look as bad as you, Rip VanWinkle's nap wouldn't even help," I chided while still trying to see how far I could push her before making her furious. At that moment, the door sprung open and I was greeted with a swift kick in the right shin—I believe I found her boiling point.

I realized that during most Christmas breaks in our part of Missouri, the weather wasn't nice enough to play outside unless you wanted to build a snowman or engage in a snowball fight. With spring training just eight weeks away, a person had to take every opportunity that the weather presented and make the most of it. Besides, knowing Missouri's weather patterns, it could be 60 degrees one day (as it was) and 20 degrees the next with freezing rain and snow.

Since I am a diehard baseball fan, I practice perfecting my game year round. Even on the days that the weather is uncooperative, I find a way to continue my practice. Because I had been confined to the basement for the previous two months, I was extremely eager to get outside and see if all the indoor practice was paying off.

37

The field conditions were a little less than favorable, but that didn't matter to me. We had received six inches of snow the week before and although it had melted, it left the ground a swampy mess. There were areas of our yard where little sprigs of green grass were popping up and also areas of just plain mud, especially around the bases.

The driest place was home plate; it was in the exact center of our sidewalk that led from the front door of our house to the garage. The width of the sidewalk was about the size of an actual batter's box. It was ideal because it never got muddy; therefore, you always had good traction when you swung the bat.

First base was the corner of our porch that extended out from the house about fifteen feet. The ground around it was a little drier than most places in our yard because it was the highest part of our yard and everything drained away from it toward third base.

Third base was the swamp of our yard. It was simply a hole in the ground. An old tree had died and my dad had had it removed, leaving a gaping hole in our front yard. For some reason, no grass would grow in the hole. I don't know how many times my father filled it with dirt and planted grass seed in it, but it didn't matter; it just remained a hole. Since it was also the lowest place in the yard, all the moisture in our yard always collected in that hole. Needless to say, it was my favorite base because it made an excellent sliding pit. I could slide into it without ever getting a strawberry (a burn on either your knee or rear end that was caused by the friction between the ground and the person sliding).

However, it was my mother's least favorite as she knew that my clothes always wound up tortured from sliding in the swamp. It was inevitable that my pants would wind up with mud streaks on the knees and grass stains on the seat. This didn't please my mother one bit. She seemed to get especially upset when I tore a hole in the knees of a pair of jeans she had already reinforced in that area. It seemed as though I ruined a pair of jeans at least once a week, or so she says. She finally bought me two pair of baseball pants just to wear when I played, so I wouldn't ruin my jeans. This made sliding even better because now I could get these pants as dirty as I wanted without getting in trouble.

The rest of the infield portion of the yard was pretty normal. Second base was a tall tree that was as close to being in line with the pitcher's mound and home plate as possible. The pitcher's mound was just a piece of trash or cardboard that was thrown to the ground and kicked into place somewhere between home plate and second base.

The outfield was another story. Just behind the infield was our lane. It was a gravel road that almost completely surrounded the infield. It entered the field from the area that I considered right field. It then wrapped its way around both second and third base in the shape of a crescent moon. On the other side of the road, was a narrow, grassy strip about ten feet wide. This strip posed as the warning track since it ran into the barbed wire fence that I considered the wall.

The fence contained dirty, smelly, rude, and ornery pigs. Yes, the place where homerun balls and ground rule doubles came to rest was a pig lot. The worst part

41

of all was that no matter how little rain or snow we had, the pig lot was always a stinking muddy mess that the pigs loved to wallow in; consequently, every time the ball entered the pig lot it always returned in worse shape than before. Even if, for some small miracle, the ball remained mud free, it always brought back a lovely manure odor with it.

Finally, after what seemed like an eternity, Andie emerged from our back porch. She slowly made her way to the home plate part of our sidewalk. On her approach, she dragged her wooden 28-inch *Louisville Slugger* baseball bat behind her. She held the knob and let the end of the barrel scrape against the cement sidewalk. This equipment torture, as I called it, caused the bat to whine in a grainy tone just as if splinters of wood were being ripped from it without proper consent.

In her right arm, she firmly held one of the leather laces that tied her mongrel-type glove together between her thumb and index finger causing the glove to dangle lifelessly by her side. Every so often, she would make a circling type motion with her arm causing the glove to twirl in a windmillish pattern.

This is exactly the reason why she had a mongrel-type glove (a cheap garage-sale-type that had replacement parts from almost every glove manufacturer). The glove was colored red in the pocket, black in the webbing, a light tan-brown on the fingers, and was laced with the most unbaseball color of all—light blue. It also emitted a musty smell that was caused by too many nights left outside in the dew or rain. Dad felt that she was too young to take care of a quality glove, so instead of buying her a new glove, he just repaired it with pieces of his old gloves that were now out of commission. That is why the glove was multicolored even though I still haven't figured out where the light blue lacing came from.

"Well, if it isn't about time," I bellowed, "we could've already played a couple of innings by now— if you weren't so slow."

"Just be glad I came out at all. Besides, Mom said if I get tired or cold to come in," taunted Andie with a look of control on her face. She knew that I couldn't play if she decided to quit. This meant that I had to put up with her and give her special advantages in order to keep her happy enough to continue playing. It also meant that she could never be losing by very much or she would quit before the game was official (four and one half innings if I were the home team or five innings if I were the visiting team).

Some of the advantages that Andie enjoyed when she batted were-I pitched a softball in slow pitch form, underhanded; she received six outs instead of three; and she could receive a walk, but she could not strike out unless it was swinging. On defense she also had a few rule revisions. She could stand as close to me as she dared and pitch the tennis ball that I had to hit, as hard as she could. I could never walk, but she could call strikes if she felt the need (which led to a few arguments). I could only hit two homeruns per inning, which, of course, I had to chase; and many times I only received one out per inning.

Feeling relieved that she had actually came out to play, I questioned, "Well, what's it gonna be, home or visitor?"

"I think I'll be the Royals!" chirped Andie.

"You village idiot! That's not what I asked. If you're the Royals, then I'm the Mariners and I can be any Mariner player that ever played for them. I also get to be the home team," I retaliated.

"Nope, I'm the Royals and I get to bat last," volleyed Andie.

"You know the way it works. You can pick one or the other, but you can't pick both the team name and when you want to bat," I responded in a patience-is-wearing-thin tone.

"I think I'm already getting tired. I'm gonna go in," smirked Andie. She knew that if I wanted to play bad enough, I would eventually give in to her requests no matter how ridiculous they might sound. Andie was good at this strategy; she seemed to use this trick quite often, and she was very successful at it.

"All right, all right, I guess you can be the home team and the Royals," I said in a quiet tone as if to look disturbed. In all actuality, this didn't bother me half as much as I tried to let her believe. I realized that we normally didn't play long enough to make the game official, so I figured that batting first wasn't that bad of a deal. At least I would get to hit before she decided to quit, which I learned in the past, was always an advantage. Too many times previously, she had quit when it came time for me to bat; but this time, she had no way out, if she wanted to bat at all.

47

Shannon Gepford

"Stepping in the batter's box is right fielder, Ichiro Suzuki. Alex Rodriguez is on deck and the dreaded Ken Griffey, Jr. is in the hole," I crooned as I took my place in the cement batter's box.

When we played, I always batted from the same side of the plate as the actual player that I was mimicking. I also repeated any distinct rituals that a player had, and if I could remember that player's stance, I copied it also. Since Ichiro Suzuki batted from the left side of the plate, I gingerly placed my left foot in the cement square that was understood to be the batter's box. I pretended to receive signs from an imaginary third base coach when Andie exploded, "Get in the box or you'll be eating this ball, 'cause I'm gonna throw it at you!"

"Well, now I'm scared. I saw you chuck numerous items at me this morning without hitting me. I don't think you could hit me if you tried 100 times," I replied without much interest.

At that moment, Andie let the tennis ball fly as hard as she could. I was frozen. The ball was on a direct flight toward my midsection. It was in one of the terrible places where a person didn't know how to move to dodge it. If I tried to duck, I would surely have been hit in the face or head. If I tried to jump, I would have been hit somewhere below the knees. The only thing that I could bring myself to do was turn my back and grimace in pain as I knew the ball was going to nail me. Sure enough, it hit me right below the rib cage on the right side of the back, just above my right kidney. It stung severely, and it left a red welt in the shape of a ball where it struck my flesh.

"Holy enchilada!" I wailed. "That baby must have had some extra hot sauce on it, 'cause it's definitely still stinging." At that point, I suddenly remembered Andie hit me with the pitch on purpose. As I glared out toward the pitcher's mound, Andie was doubled over in laughter. She had one hand over her mouth to try to hide her huge smile while the other hand was making wild gyrations in the air. In my mind, she looked as if she was the one who had been hit instead of me.

"I thought you said that I couldn't hit ya, even if I had 100 tries," squeaked Andie in between fits of laughter. Then she realized that I didn't think it was as funny as she did. The smile gradually fell from her face; it was replaced by a more solemn look that gave hints of feeling sorry for me. Unfortunately, that look didn't last very long. Almost as quickly as it came, it was gone and replaced by her normal annoying "cat-ate-the-bird-and-got-away-with-it" look.

Instead of charging the mound like some professional lunatic and making a mockery of the game, I decided to swallow my pride and let Andie enjoy her minor victory. The consequences far outweighed anything that I could have done to her. Besides, I wanted to play baseball, not get grounded by my mother for picking on Andie even if she did start the whole thing.

"Now I have a runner on first with no outs and MVP candidate, Alex Rodriguez, at the plate," I announced. I gently tapped the sidewalk with the end of my bat and proceeded to get into my batting stance on the right side of home plate. Once that was done, I turned my attention to Andie. She was pitching out of the stretch, since there was a runner on first. After checking to make sure that my ghost runner, Ichiro Suzuki, didn't have too big of a lead, she raised her left leg and right arm simultaneously. In a quick second, her right arm jutted forward, propelling the tennis ball toward my waiting bat.

Maybe the beaning I took from her earlier awoke all of the sleeping baseball instincts inside me or maybe all of the indoor practice was paying off, but whatever the case, I knew exactly how to handle that pitch. I gingerly raised my left foot to help shift my weight to meet the incoming ball. As I started to place my left foot back on the ground, the rest of my body followed forward in perfect unison. The grip that I had held loosely on the bat was now tight. My arm muscles were beginning to tighten as I pulled the bat through the strike zone in a slightly downward arc in order to insure that the bat would be level when it reached the "hitting zone" (the area where contact with the ball is made).

Meanwhile, my lower body was at work, too. My front hip was beginning to rotate toward third base, as my left foot had become planted about six inches in front of where it started. My right heel had raised off the ground, and it, too, was starting to rotate in a counterclockwise direction.

Then it happened, everything clicked into perfect harmony at the same time. The bat met the ball at the exact instant that my arms had straightened out. My

53

torso faced the pitcher's mound after such a perfect rotation that you could tie a string from my belly button to Andie's right hand, which was still dangling in front of the pitcher's mound as she tried to recover from the pitch. My right heel had also made its complete counterclockwise rotation in the same manner that you would crush a huge hissing cockroach. These movements caused all of my weight to be shifted into my swing, which in turn was shifted into Andie's pitch.

The whole event was done so smoothly; I didn't even feel the contact with the ball. The bat and ball had collided on the "sweet spot" of my 31-inch, black-stained *Louisville Slugger*. If I hadn't seen the ball literally jump off the bat, I would have sworn that I missed the pitch.

I finished my swing with the most graceful and artistic follow through ever imagined. My right hand had been released from the bat moments after contact, leaving my left hand to finish the half circle that my bat was creating. When the swing was completed, the bat head was resting near my right foot, tilted at a 45 degree angle as if to peek out from behind my right leg and observe our work. What we witnessed, was truly a remarkable piece of baseball history, especially at Spreewell County Stadium.

Chapter 3

Pig Pond

Baseball experts say, that feats like this only happen a couple times a season, and that's if you are having a good season. As I gazed toward the flight of the ball with my mouth open in amazement, time seemed to stand still. I can still remember each minor detail of the way the ball seemed to soar through the air effortlessly. At times, I even wondered if one of the immortal baseball gods had directed my body to perform this impressive event just so that he could recapture something from his glory days.

In my mind, I can still hear the dull thud that a tennis ball makes when it collides with a bat. In this

56

instance, however, the thud was louder and duller than normal. The ball had a perfect backspin rotation placed on it from its encounter with my hallowed *Louisville Slugger.* It appeared to be headed straight toward Andie's face. As it neared her enlarged cranium, the ball started to make a rapid ascent.

Later, I told her the reason the ball rose was because her Darth Vader looking face scared the ball into orbit. However, this was not the case; the backspin on the ball gave the ball lift, which turned out to be incredible. It sheltered Andie from the worst beaning possible in her short life.

The ball rose so rapidly that it completely cleared our second base tree, which stood about 30 feet tall. As the ball flew over the wall to the pig lot, it was still climbing and defying gravity. Finally, at a height I

57

estimated to be about 100 feet, the ball started to return to the earth. As it made its descent, a broad smile started to creep over my face.

"Wipe that stupid grin off your face! You could'a killed me!" fired Andie from a prone position on the ground.

"Wouldn't that have been great? I wouldn't have to put up with your mouth all the time," I rebuffed, "speaking of..., look at where it's landing."

No sooner had the words left my mouth, than the pea-green spheroid that I had launched into another area code came crashing back to earth. Its entrance could have been much more fitting, considering its majestic flight, but I didn't quibble over its only flaw. Both Andie and I cringed as we realized where the ball was destined to land—the pig pond.

Land is not an appropriate word to describe what happened to the now famous tennis ball. It struck the pig pond with such force, it buried itself in the mud next to a sleeping black and white, belted Hampshire pig, promptly awakening the sleeping beast. Its impact caused mud to spray up in all directions covering about four pigs in the immediate vicinity, which didn't seem to mind.

You see, the pig pond is not a pond at all. It is a huge mud hole at the far end of the pig lot where the pigs loved to wallow and wrestle and sleep. Unfortunately, that's not all. If the mood struck them, they would also use it as a restroom.

No ball had ever made it to the pig pond before. Some had been close but had never gotten there, partly because the pigs chased them down and tried to eat them, and partly because no ball had ever been struck with such magnitude.

Andie and I knew that we now had a difficult task to undertake. We had to retrieve the ball before the pigs found it and tried to make a meal out of it. If we didn't act fast, bad things loomed on the horizon.

First, the pigs couldn't properly digest the rubber that the tennis ball was made of. If one swallowed it, there was a possibility that it could die. Then we would have to explain to my dad what happened, which wouldn't have been much fun. Second, if a pig found it, the animal would try to chew it. Their teeth seem to ruin tennis balls rather easily, so our ball would have been demolished, and we would have had to pay for another one. Third, even if we found the ball before the pigs did, we would have to run fast;

because they thought that any time a human entered their pen, it was feeding time. Consequently, they would rub up against you and nuzzle you with their snout in hopes of receiving a meal. This always left you as dirty and smelly as the pigs were. A good trip to the pig lot usually ended with the third misfortune.

"You've got your work cut out for you. I wish you good luck in tracking down that ball," Andie whispered as she started to walk to the porch.

"What do you think you're do'un?" I questioned, "You've got to help me get that ball back."

"I planned to have a seat right here in this lawn chair and watch you chase the pigs around the pig lot. I figured it would be quite comical. Nothing better than a front row seat at a comedy event," Andie teased.

"Get your lazy, two-ton behind off that poor chair. It's gonna fold under the pressure you're puttin' on it. You've got to help me get the ball or else," I moaned.

"Or else what?" asked Andie in a very confident manner.

"Or else I'm gonna tell everyone I know that you love Twid! I heard you telling your scum-head of a friend, Jenny, how good-looking he is, and how you would do anything if he would go with you," I retorted.

"Yyoou, Yyoou, wouldn't," stammered Andie.

"Don't think I wouldn't, especially after all the rotten things that you do to me," I answered.

"You can't!" Andie groaned. "It would ruin me. The embarrassment would be too much to handle. I'd have to move to another country. I could never show my face around here again."

"Awesome!" I exclaimed, "that would be the best Christmas present ever, and I've still got two days before Christmas."

"If I help you get the ball back, you wouldn't tell, would you?" Andie squeaked in a high-pitched tone full of hope.

"Well," I drawled. "That's a tough decision—fight the pigs by myself or not have to live with Andie anymore. I think I'll pick...". Before I could finish my aloud thought, Andie had sprung from her chair and was sprinting toward the pig lot.

Realizing that Andie wasn't supposed to enter the pig lot by herself, I hurried after her. I knew that if my mom happened to come outside and Andie was in the

63

pig lot and I wasn't, then I would be in serious trouble.
I finally caught up with her just as she was starting to
climb the barbed wire fence that surrounded the pig
lot.

"Did you see exactly where it landed?" breathed
Andie as she tried to catch her breath.

"Yeah, I think so. I think that it landed just on the
other side of the black and white sow that's floppin'
'round in the mud," I answered as I pointed in the pig's
direction.

Andie was already at the top of the fence when my
problems began. Since Andie weighed far less than I
did, she was able to scale the fence without any
hesitation. Once she reached the top wire, she placed
her right hand on the top of the wooden fence post, and
in one athletic movement, she catapulted her body over

the top wire and gracefully landed on both feet in the only dry space in the entire pig lot.

"Aren't ya comin'? If ya don't hurry, that pig's gonna have a tennis ball for breakfast," Andie volleyed in hopes of making me get over the fence more quickly.

"Don't go anywhere. I'll be there in a second," I answered while trying to keep my balance without getting jabbed by one of the barbs.

It was about this time that I realized why my dad always told us to climb the fence near a fence post. Andie had followed his instructions, whether or not it was on accident I don't know, but she was already on the other side waiting on me. She hadn't had any problems getting over the barbed wire. I, on the other hand, was having fits.

Shannon Gepford

In my haste, I started my climb between two fence posts. With each step, the wire stretched and moaned under my weight. Because the wire was being stretched, it was not very sturdy. It began to sway back and forth causing me to lose my balance. In a panicked state, I grabbed for the top wire, not being careful of where I placed my hand. Sure enough, I regained my balance, but I also grasped a barb right in the middle of my palm.

Now, I was in a predicament. If I let go, the pain would go away, but then I would fall to the ground. I decided to try to bear the pain and finish my climb—what a dumb decision. After I steadied myself, I started to climb again. I was then able to release the barb and reposition my hand in another part of the wire where no barbs were sticking out.

My next movement took deft balance. I gingerly lifted my left leg and swung it over the top wire. Once it cleared the top wire, I quickly placed it back on the same wire where it had been previously resting. Now, I was straddling the top wire. I had one leg on each side of the fence, and both hands were gripped between barbs of the top wire. Because of my weight, the wire that I was standing on was starting to stretch. This unfortunate act made me stand on my tiptoes, which caused a burning sensation in my calves. I then slowly proceeded to lift my right leg when a stray barb grabbed my jeans in the most horrible place imaginable—the crotch area.

Now, I was stuck. I immediately returned my right leg to the fence in order to regain my balance. I then tried to use my left hand to pry the barb from my jeans without much luck. The wire I was standing on started making groaning sounds, so I figured that I better get off it soon, before it broke.

Meanwhile, the black and white sow had gotten up and was in the process of nosing around the area where my monumental blast had landed. "Sis, you better quit fooling around on that fence or that pig's gonna find the ball," stated Andie.

"I know, I know," was the answer I gave her in a half-hearted voice. My mind was still concentrating on how to get off the fence when suddenly the wire that I was standing on broke. All of the balance, that I had worked so hard to achieve, had left me. My weight came crashing down on the top wire. The barb that had been entwined in my jeans now was forced into the fleshy part of my right thigh. With this turn of events, I wailed, "Owww," in shear agony. My upper body sprawled forward, causing my chest to lunge toward the wire. In an effort to keep my chest from being gripped by the barbs, I leaned to the left. This desperate movement allowed my chest to miss the wire, but it also released me from any kind of balance that I may have had.

I was now in a free fall toward the ground. My head was leading the way. My eyes were closed in anticipation of landing face first in the pig lot sludge. Suddenly, my fall was interrupted. I opened my eyes and glanced around. I was hanging about six inches above the muck, upside down. My jeans were still tangled in the barb and my legs were flailing wildly.

"Help me!" I yelled. No sooner had the words left my mouth then my pants gave way. The place where

69

the barb had been holding me suspended in air started ripping my jeans because of the extra pressure that my weight had imposed on it. As my jeans ripped, I fell closer to the earth. Finally, my jeans gave way all together, and I landed face first in the sludge.

My right pant leg was ripped from the crotch to the knee, which left a gaping hole, allowing onlookers to view my Batman underwear. My right thigh and my right hand were oozing blood from their respective punctures, but worst of all, my face was covered in muck. When I looked up, the slime dripped from my face, and when I opened my mouth to speak, parts of it fell onto my lips and tongue. This made me sputter and spit in order to clear my mouth of the terrible nastiness. Without thinking, I used my left hand to try to wipe my face off. This just smeared the manure and deposited some of it in both eyes, causing my eyes to water and sting.

I must have been an awful sight. Andie had an are-you-okay-look plastered across her face. She must have thought that I was hurt, or she would have been doubled over in laughter. From a spectator's point of view, I'm sure my clumsiness would have been quite hysterical.

"Well, now that we're both in here, we might as well go find that ball," I said without opening my mouth. As we trudged along, Andie was careful where she stepped. I didn't care where I stepped. I was more concerned with wiping my face and eyes off, so I could talk without having crud slip into my mouth and see without having my eyes burn. In order for me to accomplish my chore, I had to take my shirt off and

71

use the back of it as a rag. Thankfully, it was the only place on my entire body that wasn't already covered in the smelly ooze.

Andie and I were professionals at retrieving lost balls in the pig lot. We had a system worked out. One of us would divert the pig's interest, while the other would sneak in and grab the ball. Since, I was already a mess, I was the one who had to call attention to myself. Andie would then rush over and grab the ball. Once she had it, both of us would sprint toward the nearest fence and try to get over it before the swine could reach us and nuzzle us with their snouts.

"Soohey, Soooheeey," I blurted as bits and pieces of the black nastiness was propelled from my mouth. All at once, all of the pigs stopped what they were doing and turned their heads to see what was going on.

Upon recognizing that I often fed them during chore time, they charged toward me with high hopes.

Meanwhile, Andie had crept in behind all of the animals unnoticed. She had a clear shot at retrieving the ball, if she was quick. She took off from her hidden position in a dead run toward the pig pond. She had covered about half the distance to the pond when she realized that the black and white belted sow that had been lying next to the ball was still there. The sow had been wallowing in the muck, and the muck had turned the pig's entire body the color of the pig pond. This caused the sow to be perfectly camouflaged.

The sow must have been asleep. It hadn't noticed Andie, even with all of the commotion that was going on. Andie, feeling brave, continued her trek toward the pig pond. She didn't want to startle the beast, so she slowed her pace to a more stealthy approach. Finally, she reached the edge of the pond. She peered into the mess, all the while scanning to locate the lost tennis ball. Sadly, it was not to be found.

"These pigs aren't gonna stay over here forever. Get the ball and let's git outta here," I whispered in a loud, hoarse voice.

Instead of answering me, Andie used her arms to try to convey her thoughts. First, she pointed at the pig, and then she put her index finger to her lips. I assumed that this meant for me to be quiet. Then she held both hands out to her side, brought her shoulders up toward her neck, and turned her palms upward toward the sky. With this gesture, I figured that she couldn't find the ball. Andie then started inching her way around the pond looking in every possible hole

74

and hoof print for the ball. To our dismay, it could not be found.

By now, all of the other pigs had realized that I didn't have any food. They started to wander about aimlessly when a couple of the pigs spotted Andie at the pig pond. Immediately, they broke into a dead sprint directly toward her. Andie, still searching, didn't see them coming. She was gingerly walking around, looking for the tennis ball in every possible crevice.

The two pigs that noticed her seemed to set off a chain reaction. It didn't take long before all of the pigs had bolted toward the pig pond. Oblivious to what was happening around her, Andie hadn't noticed that the rest of the swine squad was quickly closing in. I was afraid to warn her by shouting because I didn't want to wake the sow that was still sleeping, mainly because Andie was nosing around the sleeping animal.

All at once, the sleeping mud ball came to life. She jumped up in a very startled manner, which scared Andie into shock. The sow, still dazed, stared at Andie. Andie returned the sow's confused look with one of her own. Both of them, I believe, were scared to death because neither of them would move.

In the instant that the sow had jumped up, I saw the tennis ball. It had been hiding beneath the sow, in the muck that the sow had used for a bed. "Andie, grab it!" I yelled as I pointed at the tennis ball.

It was too late. My voice had brought both Andie and the sow back to reality. The sow caught a glimpse of the tennis ball before Andie and instantly reached down and picked up the mud-covered ball with its mouth, as if it were the last tasty morsel of a delicious dessert. The sow then tried to run through the muddy mess, causing mud to be slung in every direction. Of course, some of it landed on Andie.

"Yeuck!" bellowed Andie, "I should have known not to play today. This is the last time that I let you talk me into doing anything with you."

"Quit cryun' and chase down that sow before she swallows the ball," I returned while thinking about what might happen to us if the sow actually used the ball for a snack.

"My clothes are ruined thanks to you and your stupid baseball game," snapped Andie.

"Quit complaining and help me," I answered as I started chasing the black and white, belted sow.

After a few more seconds of feeling sorry for herself, Andie entered a new world—the world of muck found only in the pig pond. The clan of pigs, which both of us had forgotten about, reached her and started nuzzling her in hopes of finding food. Since, she was unprepared for their surprise attack; she was sent face first into the pig pond.

She was now covered from head to toe with the same terrible nastiness that had haunted me only a few minutes earlier. The only difference between the two of us was that she smelled worse than I did.

"I quit!" she sobbed as she slowly pulled her way out of the putrid manure.

She meant what she said. Andie was going to get out of the pig lot, and she didn't care about me, or the sow, or the rest of civilization. Realizing this, I decided not to egg her on anymore. It would only make matters worse.

Once again, I turned my attention to retrieving the tennis ball. The sow had headed for the farthest corner of the pig lot. If I was quick, I could cut the sow off and possibly get the tennis ball. I proceeded to run as fast as I could through the mud with my right pant leg flopping behind me like an uncontrollable third leg. To my amazement, I managed to cut the sow off which caused her to come to a stop.

Andie was fuming; a cluster of pigs huddled around her as she made her way back to the fence. She didn't seem to mind their presence. She was so fed up with the whole incident that she didn't acknowledge them. When she reached the fence, instead of climbing over it, she simply squeezed through it. The wire that

79

had broken from my weight had left a hole big enough for her to get through without any problems.

Now, the belted sow and I were at a standoff. Neither of us wanted to give in. Neither of us wanted to make the first move because it might have given the other one an advantage. Then, I received a piece of good fortune. The belted sow, tired from being chased, lowered her head and opened her mouth. She then began coughing, which propelled the saliva-coated, brown-stained, fuzzy, rubber tennis ball straight at me.

Being ready for anything, I caught the ball on the fly and practically flew toward the opening in the fence. My quest was not the easiest of adventures, but it paled in comparison to the things that I had already been a victim of earlier in the day. The highlights of my return trip included, sending muck flying from my feet as I ran, dodging and swerving away from hungry pigs, and squeezing through the broken fence just ahead of the caravan of hungry pigs.

Finally, both Andie and myself had reached the safety of our yard. Unfortunately, we were about to embark on an adventure far worse than what had happened in the pig lot. We still had to explain what had happened to us.

I knew that Andie would get off relatively easy. She was younger, and my parent's thought that I could convince her to do anything. My situation was extremely different. I could bet on being grounded for the rest of my Christmas break, or maybe something worse. I had broken more than a few rules, so I knew that I would have to pay the consequences. I had to face the facts. I was playing in my jeans instead of my baseball pants; I totally dismantled my jeans, possibly ruining them for life; I climbed the fence in a place where I wasn't supposed too; and I let the pigs scare Andie to death. I never thought that such a glorious day could turn out to be such a disaster.

Slowly, Andie and I slumped through Spreewell County Stadium toward our house. We walked at a speed that a turtle would admire in order to prolong our punishment. Once we reached our destination, I turned around and took one last look at the pig lot. I wanted to remember my famous clout. As I recalled the grandeur of it and the events that it had caused, I smiled. I then realized it was definitely worth whatever punishment and agony that I had faced, or would be facing.

Chapter 4

Our Sentence

Mom was outraged. If my memory serves me correctly, smoke was rising from her head and fire streaks of bright red glared in her eyes. She was so mad that the only words she could mutter were "Get cleaned up!" and "Wait til your Father gets home!"

Hesitantly, both of us started to head upstairs when mom interjected, "Hold it right there! Where in the Sam Hill do you think you're going?"

"Upstairs, to the bathroom—to get cleaned off," I responded in a quiet, questioning manner.

"Oh, no you're not! You're not going to ruin my bathroom with that pig smell. Outside, both of you," fumed my mom as she herded us out the door. "Strip and take the garden hose and spray each other off."

If you've ever been outside on a nice day in December while only wearing your underwear, you understand that the slightest breeze is enough to make you shudder and shake out of shear chilliness. Add to that unpleasant exposure, the fact that we were hosing each other off with water that had been frozen only a few days earlier. This terrible dose of cold was enough punishment for me to last a lifetime. Unfortunately, my mom didn't think our blue lips and permanently chattering teeth would be enough. After we had finished, Mom greeted us at the door with dry towels and an even drier scowl.

"Dry off and run upstairs and put some clean clothes on, and don't come down until your father gets home," she scolded.

Both Andie and I quickly dried off and made our way to our respective rooms without a sound. We knew better than to say something that would only make our predicament worse. We were too busy thinking of what our punishment would end up being and how long it would be in effect.

After what seemed like an eternity, our dad returned home from checking his cattle in a nearby field. Mom immediately filled him in on all of the morning's events. They then slowly thought out our punishment. Finally, they called both Andie and me to the kitchen.

Our time had come. We were on the verge of finding out our doom. My parents started with Andie. After scolding her about the hazards of the pigpen, she was excused. At that instant, I realized that I might have a slim chance of not being in too much trouble. Unfortunately, that thought vanished. As soon as Andie had left the room, both of my parents lit into me. They told me that I had to be the responsible one since I was the oldest. They told me that I should know better than to allow Andie into the pig lot. They told me that I shouldn't have been wearing my nice jeans that were now ruined. They told me just about everything that I had done wrong since birth, or so it seemed. Eventually, my parents tired of scolding me. They then placed the verdict of my crime in the form of a punishment.

"Solomon, you are not to watch any T.V. the rest of your Christmas break. You are also going to work with me the rest of your break doing hard, manual farm work. That means, you will be getting up at 5:00 a.m. and going to bed at 8:00 p.m. in order to be rested for the next day's work. You are also not going to Roger's New Year's Eve party," sentenced my Dad.

A blank stare came over my face; I was stunned. The part about not going to the party gouged me the most. I couldn't believe how easily Andie had gotten off. In my mind, she was as guilty as I was. I knew better than to voice my opinion about my punishment. I had learned long ago not to mess with my parent's when they were wielding the axe of punishment. They could very easily use it to dismember me from society for a very long period of time—they had in the past.

87

"By the way, Solomon, you will work every Saturday with me until you are able to pay for a new pair of jeans," smiled my Dad just as if he were pouring peroxide on a gaping wound, which he wound up doing about five minutes later. You should have heard the war hoop I gave out when that happened. Looking back, I'm glad he did disinfect my cuts, even though it was extremely painful at the time; I didn't get any infections, which would have been worse.

Once I was cleaned up and bandaged, I put on my work clothes in order to start filling my death sentence. On my way out the door, my dad laid his heavy hand on my shoulder and whispered in my ear, "I wish I could've seen the hit; it must have been awesome." He then winked at me and smiled a warm smile to give me a sense of pride and worth even in this time of upcoming hard, manual labor.

My hard, manual labor consisted of fixing the fence to the pig lot, scooping manure out of the pig pens that housed new mothers and their offspring, feeding hay to the cattle, and any other chore that needed to be done on or around the farm. When my stint as a farmer ended, I was truly relieved. I had worked hard, and I felt good about finishing my task even though it was a punishment that I had to fulfill. Although I missed the best party of the decade, or so I was informed when I returned to school, I still wouldn't trade my majestic mash of a homerun and the consequences it brought for anything in the world.

"Heard you scooped poop, or should I say the poop was scooped on you," bellowed Carlos in a tone that indicated he was glad to see me. "Wish I coulda seen you runnin' round the yard freezin' to death in your undies," continued a hysterically cackling Carlos.

Not having much to say, I decided to try to ignore this moron, but with a person that spits as he talks, ignoring him is like taking a shower and not getting wet—impossible. When Carlos gets excited, he talks faster and faster and spittle flies from his mouth at an uncontrollable bubbling rate. Consequently, I couldn't ignore the spit that landed on the tip of my nose even if I could have ignored his badgering.

"Say it! Don't spray it!" I muttered as I wiped the wet spot from my nose with the back of my hand.

At this point, Carlos became unnerved. His one major physical flaw was a constant aggravation for him, and it embarrassed him to no end. I now had him cornered like a nervous animal. He would do or say anything to get out of the corner and focus the attention back on me instead of his spitting problem. Luckily, the bell rang for class to begin and everyone started filing to their seats.

Looking back, I think both of us were relieved that our conversation ended without either of us getting into a fight or at the very least embarrassed any further. Besides, I had more important things to worry about than Carlos' spitting problem. Roger had informed me that at his party, Chris Scofield kept asking questions about me. That tidbit of information meant one of two things. Either she felt really sorry for me or she had a *crush* on me and was sad that I wasn't there. I didn't care which was the case since this woman had secretly been the object of my affection since second grade.

Just to have her thinking about me was enough to put me in a good mood. I knew; however, I would have to play it cool in order to win the affections of this fifth grade, **Sports Illustrated**, swimsuit model. That's right! If her body continued to develop at its current pace, she would make Britney Spears look like a super model wannabe, and if I played my cards right, this would be my year for love.

Chapter 5

Chris Scofield & Lunch Room Cockroach

Thanks to Roger and his before school briefing, I was on top of the world. I had even caught Chris sneaking small peeks at me. Each time that I would catch her, she would give me a great big smile and blush. Oh, how I loved it when she blushed. When she blushed, her face turned bright red as she tilted her head to the side as if she was trying to disappear through the neck hole of her blouse. Every time she did this action the collar on her blouse would partially cover her left cheek, and a teasing grin would encompass her beautiful face. This body language told me that I definitely had her interest and that she

93

wanted to be caught peeking at me because every time I caught her she quickly looked away. Then, after a slight hesitation, she would look back at me again to make sure that I was still looking at her.

After careful analysis of the situation, I decided to make an extremely bold move for me. Since I was feeling as self-confident as humanly possibly, I figured that I couldn't go wrong. I decided to break the lead in my pencil on purpose so I would have to get out of my seat to sharpen it. Going to the pencil sharpener, meant walking directly past Chris. I had planned to say something cute yet teasing to let her know that I was also in the game.

Unfortunately, I wasn't the only one that noticed Chris' sudden infatuation with me. Roger, who never let anything by without his awareness; picked up on

Chris' behavior, too. Without my knowing, Roger had been devising a plan that would put Chris and me together as the perfect couple. His new occupation as Cupid probably should have been named Stupid upon looking back at the confusion, embarrassment, and trouble that he caused me.

Once out of my seat, I started striding to the pencil sharpener. Between my desk and Chris' I was met with a hoarse whisper coming from Roger's throat, "Hey Dude! That babe's been starin' at you all mornin'. Go say somethun to her. She wants you man. Trust me, I know."

"SHhhhh! The whole class can hear you and now Chris is looking over here. Besides I've got a plan," I quipped.

"Oh, that lame idea about going to the pencil sharpener and saying something cute. Nice try, but everyone does that. You need something better in order to bag that hot lookin' doe," stated Twid in a hoarse undercover whisper that could be heard clear across the room.

"How did you know that was my plan?" I questioned. "Besides, could you be any louder? Mrs. Bussitt down the hall wouldn't even have to turn up her hearing aid in order to hear you."

At this time, Mrs. Sauerborn gave us a quick glare that said, "Shut Up! Sit Down! Get to Work!" all in one. It amazed me how she could get all of her points across without even uttering a word, but both of us knew exactly what she meant. I then continued to the pencil sharpener but decided against saying anything cute to Chris. Instead, I just gave her a friendly smile and a quick wink, and then I returned to my seat immediately after sharpening my pencil. I knew it was almost time for recess and it was still football season. I had to be ready to burst out the door and run to the field in order to claim it so we could play before the sixth graders got there.

Luckily, we won the race to the field, so we got to play football on this cool, crisp January morning. After choosing sides, I caught a glimpse of Chris standing on the sidelines of the field. She must have come to watch me play I thought as my mind began to swell. The swelling then spread to my face and a huge grin broke over it. It was so big it hurt. I think I could have even eaten a banana sideways. All the while, we were getting ready for the kickoff since we were the receiving team.

My pleasant thoughts were interrupted with the bombarding voice of Carlos, "Well, Loverboy, are you ready to play? If we're gonna win, we can't have you starun' at Chris."

"Yeah!"chimed Frank.

"What do ya mean?" I quivered, afraid that my secret was not so secret anymore.

"The whole class knows that Chris has the hots for you, and you're so lovesick you think that no one saw you wink at her," boomed Carlos.

"You winked at Chris?" squeaked Louis.

"Yes, you idiot, he did. It was mighty cute too, I might add, since he got her to blush," announced Carlos.

"I didn't wink at her. I had something in my eye. Besides I can prove I'm not in love with her," I boasted.

"Now, how are you gonna do that?" questioned Carlos.

"I won't look at or talk to Chris the rest of the day," I replied.

Once said, the rest of the group thought that that announcement would be sufficient for them to start open season on me if I slipped up-or if I didn't slip up, then maybe I was telling the truth. Knowing what I had just done, I felt sick because I knew I couldn't win this game. I was either going to tick Chris off and lose the possibility of "going with" a fifth grade super model, or I was going to be verbally humiliated by every guy that knew me.

99

I played the game of my life. I could do no wrong. Every time I did something well, Chris cheered. The more she cheered, the better I played, but I couldn't even acknowledge her existence. I was afraid of losing face and this dilemma bothered me. We did crush Roger's team so all was not lost—but I needed help.

"Twid," I breathed while lining up to go in from recess. "I need help. I can't look or talk to Chris the rest of the day or I'll lose face."

"Have no fear, Sis, my dear. I figured you would get yourself in some kind of mess, so I've already devised a plan to help you out in your budding relationship with Chris. Leave everything to me—it's taken care of," assured Twid.

"I don't know what your plan is, but all I need for you to do is to tell Chris about the deal that I made and that I am not playing hard to get," I begged.

"I've got it under control. Don't worry, Chris will be eating out of the palm of your hand by tomorrow morning, and you won't have to do a thing," reassured Twid.

"I wish I had your confidence right now," I muttered as I had a horrible feeling about the whole situation.

Once in class, Roger began working on his master plan. His mind was racing and he had that crinkled eyebrow-flared nose look. That didn't help my nervousness. I still had a terrible gut feeling that something had to go wrong with his plan even though I didn't know what his plan was. Every once in a while,

I would catch him writing something down on a sheet of paper and then he would go back into deep thought.

Finally, it was time for lunch. I wasn't hungry because my stomach was wrapped up in knots. My mind wasn't focusing on class work; I had bigger worries—what Roger's plan was, and if it would work, and what Chris was thinking of me since I hadn't looked at her or spoken to her since before the football game.

"Your plan, it working?" I quizzed in a desperate tone.

"It's about to go into action. You'll see, your troubles are over, Solomon. By this time tomorrow, you'll be the talk of the school, ya know Big Man on Campus type stuff," crooned an ever proud Twid.

At lunch I made sure to sit at a table next to the one Chris sat at. I also made sure that my back was to her, so I wouldn't be tempted to look at her. I made Roger sit across from me so he could have a perfect view of Chris; therefore, he could inform me of anything that she did that might have an impact on my newfound relationship.

We were served little smokies, scrambled eggs, spinach, a peanut bar, and a pear half. What a disgusting meal! First of all, little smokies are miniature sausages that are great with eggs for breakfast, not for lunch. Spinach is not good for any meal. The peanut bar and pear half were about the only things that were edible on our trays. What a nutritious meal—peanut bar and a pear half.

Shannon Gepford

Out of all the kids in our class only two ate everything on their tray. The rest of us starved the remainder of the day. Besides the nasty food, a huge, one-legged cockroach was found under D.B.'s pear half. This unexpected surprise put a fine finish to everyone's lunch.

"Well, would you look at that!" shouted D.B. "A freakun' roach was hidin' under my pear! Hey he's only got one leg."

"It's nice to know the quality of lunches served around here," added Carlos.

"Let me see," giggled Louis as he squirmed in for a closer view. "You know, those things carry diseases. It could have infected all of us."

"Cool your jets, Man. This thing ain't gonna hurt us. It's just a bug. Anyone have five bucks they would give me if I ate this creature?" pronounced D.B.

"I do!" yelled Frank, "but only if you eat it in five pieces. You have to cut it up and eat it piece by piece. You have to have the first piece swallowed before you stick another one in your mouth."

"No sweat! I get a dollar per piece," exclaimed D.B. "Shake and you're on, Moneybags. Making money the easy way, I ought to tell the lunch ladies to give me surprises more often so I can earn some extra cash for dippin'," muttered D.B. as he prepared his protein power bug for digestion.

"You guys are disgusting!" shrieked Gretchen grabbing her side as if it gave her a pain. Funny thing though, she inched closer and closer to the action to witness the feeding.

News of the bet traveled fast in the lunchroom. Before D.B. had finished cutting his roach into five distinct pieces, everyone started scampering into positions in which they could view the event. Roger, knowing everybody would probably overlook his actions, took this opportunity to slip Chris a note. He stealthily glided over to Chris' table, and when D.B. took his first bite, Roger carefully slipped the note into the pocket of her jacket. At the same time he was giving her the note, he whispered instructions in her ear. Roger then walked back to our table unnoticed like the cool, suave and debonair James Bond after completing a mission.

"Mission accomplished," he breathed.

By now D.B. was devouring the last piece of cockroach. He was enjoying his meal so much, that he was making sure that everyone could hear the crunching sounds his teeth were making upon grinding the cockroach into digestible pieces. He did save the leg for dessert. After eating the five pieces to win the wager, he cleansed his palate with the cockroach's only leg as he glanced around the room for approval.

"Frankie, oh Frankie—it's time to pay up," smiled D.B. with a piece of cockroach still stuck to one of his front teeth.

"You're beyond help," needled Frank as he handed D.B. the money.

"Nice do'un business with ya," smirked D.B. as he folded the money while sticking it into his pocket.

Shannon Gepford

"At least get that bit of cockroach that's stuck to your tooth removed," added Frank as he turned to walk away.

By now, lunch was over and everyone was putting up their trays and filing into line in order to head back to class. Even though it was extremely hard to keep from looking at Chris, I somehow managed to keep my willpower in tact. With Roger's help, I was able to get back to class and seated without noticing Chris.

Chapter 6

"Going with"...

The afternoon seemed to creep by. I caught myself staring at the clock on numerous occasions. I hadn't had the chance to find out what Roger told Chris or what he wrote on the note that he slipped her. Finally, two o'clock came and we lined up to go to art. I knew that I would find out exactly what was going on during art because Roger and I sat next to each other, and we were working on a paper mâché dinosaur together.

"Hey, what's going on?" I questioned as we took our seats in the art room.

"I just gave Chris a little note; that's all," teased Roger.

"Don't tease me," I whined. "I've worried all day, and I need to know what's going on."

"All right, I'll tell you. The note explained why you're giving her the silent treatment and that you could explain things to her further if she met you behind the football tower before school tomorrow morning. I really impressed myself this time. I wrote it as if it came from you, and when I delivered it to her, I whispered that I was only the messenger boy," informed Roger with an extremely proud look on his face.

"Is that all the note said?" I quizzed while still feeling a slight bit uneasy.

"I also wrote that you wanted to "go with" Chris, and if she showed up in the morning you guys would be a couple. If she didn't show up, then that meant that she didn't want to "go with" you. Either way you can't lose in this game. You will have fulfilled your promise to the guys, and by tomorrow afternoon, you will be the envy of everyone in the school. By the way, I didn't put Chris' name on the note in case it fell into the wrong hands," stated Twid in his undercover detective voice as he dipped a piece of newspaper in the milky glue and proceeded to slap it on our replica of T-Rex.

Momentarily, my anxiety subsided. It sounded to me as if Twid had handled the situation extremely well and that I was still in the game with less than an hour of school left before I took the bus home. Then it hit me. My anxious feelings returned. What if Chris decided not to meet me tomorrow morning? What if I misread her blushes? What if she really didn't want to

Shannon Gepford

"go with" me after all and she was just flirting? What if my parents found out? If the answer to any of these questions were not what I was hoping for, I would be under severe embarrassment—what a blow to my self-esteem. At this point, I knew my nervousness wouldn't leave until after the moment of truth— tomorrow morning.

The rest of the day went by as easily as I could have hoped considering my stressful situation. The bus ride home was uneventful as usual. Andie even left me alone. It was almost like she could tell something was bothering me. Once home, I flipped on the T.V., made myself a ham sandwich to take the place of my missed lunch, and poured myself a tall glass of chocolate milk. I then sauntered to the couch and comfortably sat down. Within minutes, I had

112

devoured my makeshift meal and was asleep on the couch.

"Time for dinner," yelled my Mom.

Upon hearing those magic words, I was immediately awakened from my slumber. I groggily sat up and tried to get my bearings. Just then, Andie whizzed by and slapped me on the head. Before I could register what had happened, she was past me and into the safety of the kitchen. I let the slap slide this time as I figured it was a battle that I could not win, and I didn't want to put out the effort to fight.

"How was school today?" Mom asked.

"Okay," was my reply as I slowly rose from the couch.

"Anything exciting happen today that you want to tell me about?" quizzed my Mother.

"Nnnnoo," I stammered. "Why, did you hear something?"

"No, I just thought you might have some new and exciting news," replied my mom.

Maybe she could tell I was hiding something or maybe it was just a coincidence, but I was relieved when my dad walked through the door so the conservation could be switched from me. I made it through the rest of dinner unscathed. I then hurriedly put my dishes away and rushed upstairs. I hoped to be left alone with my thoughts for the rest of the evening.

Morning came earlier than expected. I tossed and turned all night. I was torturing myself with negative thoughts about the upcoming meeting with Chris. It seemed as though I had just gotten to sleep when the alarm went off and rudely awakened me. After going through my normal morning routine, I was on my way to the bus with Andie tagging along behind.

Once on the bus, I chose a seat directly over one of the wheels. I tossed my backpack into the seat and then I flopped down next to it. After about a twenty-minute drive, the bus stopped at Roger's house. This was strange. Roger never rode the bus. His mother worked at a floral shop right across the street from the school. He always rode to school with her so he could sleep a little longer.

When the bus slowed to a halt, I could see Roger lugging his trombone case in one hand and his backpack in the other. He really struggled as he tried to make his way through the bus door. Once inside, he started making his way down the aisle to my seat.

"Oooowww!" yelled Andie. "Would you watch what you're doin' with that thing?"

"Sorry, I didn't mean…," apologized Roger.

"That's okay, Roger," interrupted my sister as she realized that it was her fantasy man that smacked her on the head with a trombone case. "I know it was an accident."

"Way to go, Twid. You can definitely tell you're not a veteran bus rider. By the way, we don't have band today, so why the trombone?" I questioned.

"Just part of my plan for you and Chris," answered Roger as he plopped down next to me.

"What ya gonna do? Play music at our rendezvous," I chided sarcastically.

"No, you idiot. Look what I brought for you," he boasted as he opened the lid to the trombone case.

Roger had stolen three bright red roses from his mom's rose garden. Roger's mother had a greenhouse connected to the side of his house. She grew numerous types of plants and flowers all year long in it. Roger had decided that to make my plan effective he would steal these flowers for me so I could give them to Chris this morning.

Since I couldn't read the Twid's mind, I questioned hesitantly, "What are those for?"

"Sis, you're going to give Chris two of these at your meeting when you ask her to "go with" you. The other one is for Mrs. Sauerborn. That way if someone spies you carrying one, you'll be off the hook when they later see it on Mrs. Sauerborn's desk. The plan is for you to drop one off with a note saying 'Thanks for being such a great teacher, signed Solomon' on Mrs.

Sauerborn's desk before your meeting with Chris. You then wrap the other two in your coat so nobody sees them and head to your encounter with Chris. Once you're there, give her the roses and you'll be THE MAN!" stated Roger.

"Sounds okay, but what is Chris gonna do with the roses after I give them to her? Besides, they're all smashed from your trombone," I inquired.

"The roses will be all right when they get some fresh air. As for Chris, tell her to hide them in her coat until after school. Then, she can show anyone she wants," informed Roger.

"Great plan, I hope it works as well as you make it sound," I mumbled as my stomach found places that hadn't previously been tied in knots.

Before long, the bus slowed to a stop at the school and all of us departed to start another day. I quickly made my way to our classroom with Roger tagging closely behind. Luckily, I was the first one there. I rushed over to Mrs. Sauerborn's desk, opened my coat, pulled out a rose, scribbled down Roger's predetermined message, and turned to leave just as Carlos and Oscar entered the room.

"Whew, that was close," I murmured as I blew past Roger on my way to my date with Chris.

"Good luck!" the Twid blurted in reply.

I reached the tower before Chris did. I was slightly relieved since the first part of the plan seemed to be working to perfection. From that point on though, everything seemed to unravel and fast.

"Gretchen!" I screamed. "What are you doing here?"

"Coming to meet my honey," she answered while pulling out the note that Roger had given to Chris the day before at lunch.

"Hhooooowww, ddiid yyyoouuu get that?" I stuttered.

"From you silly, it was laying under my chair in the art room. Are those for me?" she asked as she suddenly noticed the roses that I had clenched in my right fist.

The note must have fallen out of Chris' pocket as she left the art room yesterday. Unfortunately, it fell in a place that was proving to be very unsettling to my nerves. I stood there for what seemed to be an eternity trying to grasp the situation at hand and how I could remedy it as quickly and easily as possible.

"Well, Sis, are those roses for me?" pushed Gretchen.

Gretchen's voice brought me back into the present verbally but not mentally as I responded with "Certainly, I hope you like them."

At that instant, Gretchen rushed over to me, scooped the roses from me, and planted a great big kiss and hug on me all in the same motion. Simultaneously, I saw Chris out of the corner of my eye, turn and walk away. My heart sank. Thoughts raced through my mind: The woman of my dreams must think I'm a big loser. Gretchen loves me. Now I've got a bigger mess to get out of than ever before.

"I love you, Solomon Isaiah Spreewell," whispered Gretchen in my ear as she also turned to head to class.

To understand the magnitude of my problem, you must first understand a little bit about Gretchen. Gretchen was the biggest person in our class. She looked like one of those Amazon women that I had heard of. She was the loudest, most obnoxious girl in the whole school. She always got her way; plus she got everything that she ever wanted since her parents owned most of the land in our county and had plenty of money left over to buy anything they wanted. I can't think of anyone that really liked her. Most of us just kind of tolerated her. She could, at times, annoy the paint completely off the wall with her constant whiny voice and stupid attention seeking questions. Plus, she had fire red hair, a slight mustache above her upper lip, braces, and an overactive acne problem for a fifth grader.

It was official. I was now "going with" my first woman and it was awful. My first girlfriend and I got the wrong one by mistake. I had been the victim of extremely bad luck and now I had to suffer the consequences.

Chapter 7

Kisses

"Yahooo, Romeo!" yelled Oscar at the top of his lungs upon my return to the classroom.

"We had it all wrong boys. Loverboy here wasn't after Chris after all. He was smooth talkin' big 'ol tall Godzilla Gretchen," bellowed Carlos.

"Godzilla Gretchen-that's good Carlos, but I was thinkin' more on the lines of the Bride of Frankenstein," heehawed D.B.

I walked past the henchmen as quickly as I could and sat down in my seat. I wanted to hide under my desk. After a few seconds, I raised my head and saw the whole class giggling at me except for Gretchen who was beaming wildly and Chris who blushed just as she had the day before when this whole mess started. Upon further investigation of the classroom, I noticed Chris' flowers that I had given to Gretchen were in a small glass vase on the corner of Gretchen's desk. Now I knew for sure that everyone knew who I was "going with".

"How could I ever get out of this jam?" I asked myself. I definitely wouldn't be requesting the Twid as my love counselor anymore. Upon reflecting over the incidents that took place before school, I began to rationalize why I acted the way I did. As much as I disliked the way Gretchen treated people, I couldn't be mean to her. Everyone else was mean and unfriendly to her and I knew that if people treated me like that then I would probably treat them the same way in return. I guess I kind of felt sorry for her. She didn't have any close friends so maybe this one act of being nice, even though it went against my better judgement, might help her to be nice to other people and then maybe the other people would return the favor to her.

Now, how could I "break up" with Gretchen without totally crushing her heart and leaving her meaner and nastier than ever and still be nice about it? I knew I couldn't "go with" someone that I didn't really like. I just had to be gentle when I let her down.

I spent most of the rest of the day trying to figure out a way to accomplish this unpleasant task. Most of the day I eluded insults, but when one did find its mark, I just laughed along with the sender. When you're being made fun of, if you laugh too, people don't tend to keep making fun of you. I guess it isn't any fun for them if they think it doesn't bother you. I did, however, try to dodge as many conversations as possible.

With about ten minutes left in class, Mrs. Sauerborn stated, "Solomon I need to see you after class for a couple of minutes."

Now, what had I done? It was probably something to do with the flowers that I had given Gretchen. Since I wasn't riding the bus home, I could stay for quite a while, which would allow all the henchmen to leave without giving me any parting barbs.

Suddenly, the bell rang to dismiss us from school. I stayed at my desk as all the other students packed up their things to go home. I said goodbye to Gretchen and Roger and Louis and Frank and even Chris (she

127

smiled) as I waited to see what Mrs. Sauerborn wanted
to talk to me about.

"Solomon," started Mrs. Sauerborn, "I want to
thank you for the beautiful rose you gave me this
morning, but I didn't want to do it in front of the class.
I figured you had enough heckling for one day."

"You're welcome and thank you," I replied.

"Roger told me of your plan and I think it was very
sweet of you to want to give Chris flowers," continued
Mrs. Sauerborn.

"But…" I started.

"Roger was worried that you would be late for
class. He warned me you were in an awfully important
meeting. I then forced him to tell me the whole story.
I now know everything from start to finish. I figured
something had gone wrong when I saw Gretchen

heading toward the tower while Chris was just getting

off her bus," Mrs. Sauerborn added.

"You knew about the meeting, your flower, Chris

not Gretchen," I pondered aloud in amazement.

"I knew about the whole thing, thanks to Roger,"

she replied. "I would also like to add that if I was

Chris I would be extremely impressed because you

didn't embarrass Gretchen when you easily could

have. You showed a maturity that most fifth graders

don't have and if Chris is smart she will realize it too."

"But what about Gretchen?" I asked in a confused

tone.

"I think that problem is taking care of itself,"

announced Mrs. Sauerborn as she motioned with her

head toward the door.

129

Outside the door were Gretchen and Louis. They seemed to be waiting for me. The way this day had gone I couldn't dream of what was next.

"Got a minute," boomed Gretchen in her I'm in charge voice.

"Yeah, what's up?" I asked.

"I'm gonna give it to you straight," started Gretchen. "You see I've had a major crush on Louis for a long time. When I found your note, I was momentarily blinded by your good boy image. Let's face it, Sis. I like a man who lives on the edge-like Louis here. I guess what I'm saying is that I want to "break up" with you so I can "go with" Louis. I hope I didn't hurt your feelings too bad. By the way the flowers were beautiful, but if you want a woman like me, a Sammy Sosa rookie card would have worked better."

"Well," I stammered "if that's the way you feel then that's okay. I wish you and wild man Louis the best of luck. Louis take good care of her."

"You better believe I will," squeaked Louis.

"C'mon Louis, let's go," barked Gretchen as she almost yanked Louis' right arm out of its socket.

"I love it when she takes control," squeaked Louis once again.

As they turned to head off down the hall I chuckled to myself. Louis was about half the size of Gretchen. Gretchen was practically dragging Louis, as he had to jog to keep up with her long strides. Shoot, she even had a deeper voice than he did. They would make a perfect couple.

Feeling a little better, I turned back into the classroom. Mrs. Sauerborn was smiling.

Oddly, she knew the outcome long beforehand.

"Mrs. Sauerborn, you're the greatest!" I announced, as I was suddenly feeling much more relieved.

"Solomon, I want to give you this rose," stated Mrs. Sauerborn as she handed me the rose that I had placed on her desk earlier that morning. "You are a very noble young man. You are a knight in shining armor to some lucky young lady. You are the consummate gentleman."

I started to blush and put my head down as I breathed, "Thank you."

"You may just need this," she whispered as she softly placed a kiss on my cheek.

I slowly grabbed my books and headed toward the door when to my surprise, Chris was standing there. Once again, she was blushing with her collar half hiding her beautiful smile. This time her eyes were sparkling more than normal.

"Solomon," she gasped. "I wanted you to know that what you did for Gretchen this morning was the nicest thing that I have ever seen. She must have found my note, cause when I got home it wasn't in my pocket anymore."

"You mean you weren't upset that I gave her your flowers?" I asked.

"No way. You spared her feelings and that makes you more of a man than any girl can dream of. I would like to be your girlfriend if you still want one," Chris pleaded.

133

"That would be AWESOME!" I shouted before I realized that I needed to control my excitement.

I then reached for her hand and gently, placed the third generation rose in her palm. I then gave a quick glance back at Mrs. Sauerborn who gave me a smile and a quick wink.

I returned the smile to Mrs. Sauerborn and turned my head back to face Chris just in time to receive my third kiss of the day.

"Congratulations!" yelled the Twid from across the hall.

"How long have you been there?" I asked gruffly.

"Long enough," responded the Twid. "I love it when a plan comes together."

"Some plan, it almost blew up and caused terrible damage," I volleyed.

"But it didn't. Anyway, look at you now, the beautiful super model, and the Big Man on Campus holding hands and going together," stated an extremely proud of himself Roger.

"By the way, I gave Sadie your phone number and told her to call you," I teased.

"You didn't," trailed Twid.

Who knows, maybe this year would be a year to remember after all.

Chapter 8

What is the Capitol of Missouri?

Now that I had a real, live girlfriend, I had to act like I deserved one. That meant that I should get to work making some money in case I ever got a chance to be alone with Chris. Therefore, I could pay for a soda or candy bar or something else. The only problems with this thinking were that first I probably would only be alone with Chris at one of our high school's basketball games. Second, our parents' brought us to these games since neither of us could date and third, the only job that I could get was baby pig midwife.

Being a baby pig midwife is a rough job. A person has to set his alarm for crazy hours in the middle of the night. Then, get up, put on cold weather clothing (since baby pig midwives are only needed during the coldest months of the year), run to the farrowing house, and check the pregnant sows to make sure that they weren't having any piglets. If the sows weren't 'piggin', then one could run back to the house and go back to bed and repeat the process the next time the alarm went off. If the sows were 'piggin', then you stayed there and acted like a catcher getting ready to receive a pitch from Boston Red Sox hurler, Pedro Martinez.

What I mean is that you open up the door to the farrowing crate that housed the pregnant sow. You then grabbed a towel and dried off any of the newborn babies that the sow already had. Once you had them dry, you held them close to your body to warm them up by your body heat. If there were more than two already born, you simply stuffed the little pigs into the pockets of your coveralls until they quit shivering. When they quit shivering you placed them under a heat lamp to keep them warm and guided them to their mother's breast so they could suck milk that would give them extra energy to fight the cold of the night. You then sat on a white five-gallon bucket that was turned upside down and waited for the next one to arrive so you could start the procedure over again.

The thought of getting up in the middle of the night and freezing did not appeal to me, but if that was going to be my only source of income, then I would easily handle the unpleasantness so I could make Chris happy. Besides, being a baby pig midwife wasn't all that bad. I got to witness the miracle of life on numerous occasions, which is truly awesome. I also made $.25 for every baby pig that I was able to keep alive. Normally, a sow had 12-15 baby pigs per litter, which translated into a minimum of $3.00 for a couple hours work. The best part was that I had CASH! I could buy my sweetie a snack at the game and feel proud about it.

"How many did 'ol Snake have last night?" questioned my Dad as he greeted me at the breakfast table as I was returning from the farrowing house.

"Seventeen!" I exclaimed excitedly.

"She sure is a good 'ol sow," answered my Dad in a trailing off tone.

"One of the best. Because of her, I'm gonna collect $4.25 from ya for my sleepless night," I crowed.

Dad had moved on to other things but I could tell by the look on his face that he was happy. He was happy that Snake had so many babies because that meant increased profits for him in the long run and he was proud of me for working hard to make sure that none of her baby pigs died. Even though my dad didn't always tell me how proud of me he was, I could usually tell. This was one of those times. I knew that I had done well and he didn't have to say a word because the look on his face and 'his actions were enough of a compliment to me.

My next obstacle to overcome was getting to the basketball game on Friday night. My dad enjoyed going to the games if they could fit into his tight schedule—he was a workaholic. I decided to start working on him early in the week to convince him we needed to go on Friday. I told him how important this game was and how it was simply a "must see".

Getting Chris to the game was no problem. Her parents were always there. I don't think they ever missed a game. They even traveled to faraway games in places like Fenway or Camden. Both of those towns were over an hour away on dangerous, curvy roads. They had a reason to be there. Chris had twin brothers. Her brothers were in the tenth grade, but they played on the varsity basketball team. They were actually the best players on the team and I both admired and liked them. They were my kind of guys.

"Go'un to the game on Friday?" asked Louis the Wednesday morning before the game.

"I hope to," I replied in an anxious tone.

"I'm go'un," squeaked Louis in a pitch that I had never heard him reach before, "this'll be my first game this year and guess who I get to go with—Gretchen the love of my life—Oh, by the way, thanks fer a ya know."

I nodded, as I understood exactly what Louis was thanking me for. I probably should have been thanking him for taking Gretchen away from me instead of vice versa.

"Hey Sis! Are you go'un to the big game?" shouted Roger from across the room.

Once again I gave the same reply, "I hope to."

"You better, or I'll have to keep your babe warm," sputtered D.B. as he interrupted Roger before Roger could make a wise remark of his own.

"That's right, Sissy my boy," gargled Carlos with a breath so stinky it would make even a dead, bloated piece of road kill roll over twice to get away from it, "Me and D.B. will take good care of her in your absence. Hope ya have fun at home on Friday."

"Man, what have you been eating-did you brush your teeth this week?" exclaimed Roger.

"Yes, idiot, I brushed them yesterday, whether they needed it or not and for your information, I had and am still eating an omelet filled with liverwurst, jalapenos, and other special ingredients," spit Carlos as he reached into his pocket and pulled out his half-eaten omelet.

"Put that thing away!" Roger and I yelled in unison, "It smells worse than your breath," finished Roger.

Just then, the bell rang for class to begin. All of us scattered to our seats as Mrs. Sauerborn was about ready to start class. It had snowed a lot the night before and many of the buses had not arrived at school yet. Of course, mine would have no trouble, but Chris' bus wasn't to school yet. Mrs. Sauerborn had us proceed anyway just like everyone was there.

I couldn't help it, but my mind was wandering. I knew I had to get to the game for sure now. If the henchmen were going to be there, along with Louis, Gretchen, Roger, and who knew whom else, I just had to find a way to make sure I was at the game if for no other reason than to protect Chris.

"Solomon, Solomon! What is the capitol of Missouri?" Mrs. Sauerborn asked, as she knew I wasn't paying attention.

"Chris," I replied without thinking.

Instantly, the class erupted into thunderous laughter. I had been caught daydreaming and now everyone knew it. My face had already turned bright red from embarrassment, but there was no where to hide.

"I mean, Jefferson City," I stuttered while trying to save as much dignity as I could.

Mrs. Sauerborn definitely got her point across about paying attention and she didn't have to say another word. She just gave me a look to let me know things could be worse than being embarrassed, but at that time I didn't know how they could be.

145

Chapter 9

Go'un to the Game?

The rest of the day at school was awful. Chris' bus didn't arrive until 1:00 p.m. and the superintendent decided to let school out at 1:15 p.m. That meant that I didn't get to see Chris, since she didn't get off her bus. Her bus basically turned around and left. Besides that "downer," I was constantly abused by my classmates with insulting remarks about my obvious day dreaming in class earlier that morning.

"Chris! I mean Sis," shouted Roger as he heckled me down the hall on our way to the bus.

"Aw, go kiss your fat uncle's corn infested, pus watering, athlete's foot carry'un pinky toe," I blurted.

"Testy, aren't we, Sis?" quizzed Roger with a smirk that would annoy the bark off a tree.

"Wouldn't you be?" I returned.

With my last remark, Roger could tell that I wasn't in the mood for his playful kidding. He wisely wished me a "good evening" and a "things will be better tomorrow" as he noticed his mother standing at the bus to take him home so he wouldn't have to ride the bus in the bad weather.

The ride home on the bus gave me time to think of a way to get to the basketball game on Friday. Unfortunately, it didn't help. The best plan I could come up with was simply begging. I knew that idea was pretty lame, since my dad would probably see through the idea and find a reason to stay home. Finally, after wrestling with trying to find a way to get

147

to the game, I decided to act like a man and just come right out and tell him that I would like to go to the game.

"Dad, can we go to the basketball game at school on Friday?" I asked with a tone that had a questioning air.

"Maybe, why do you want to go?" Dad answered with a question of his own.

"All of my friends are going to be there," I spouted with enthusiasm.

"That shouldn't matter," he responded, "you need to be your own person and not let what everyone else is doing influence you. You need to be your own man."

"I am my own man. I would just like to go to the game. We haven't been to a game all year and it's supposed to be a good game and I've worked hard with the pigs and," I was stating as my Dad cut me off.

"We'll try to go," he answered, "I would like to see those twins play-I hear they're pretty good for as young as they are."

"Thanks, Dad! I can't wait!" I shouted as I raced up the stairs in a mood that was different than the mood that I had been in for most of the day.

If I knew getting to go to the game was to be this easy, I wouldn't have had to worry about it at all. I should have realized it sooner. All I needed to do was to face my small problem head on and see what the outcome was. It suddenly clicked-my parents had been trying to teach me that simple lesson since birth with biblical stories. The one story that was now sticking out in my mind was the story of David and Goliath.

149

David met his much larger problem (Goliath) head on and David was the victor because of it. He didn't spend needless time worrying about it, he just took care of his problem (Goliath). I wish I handled my much smaller problem the way David did. It would have saved me a lot of upset stomach time.

"Hey D.B.!" bellowed Oscar, "What's the capitol of Missoura?

"CCCcchris!" stuttered D.B. in a mocking tone as both he and Oscar burst into a high pitched hysterical laughter.

"It's good to know you clodhoppin' goons will get at least one of the capitol test questions right thanks to me. Actually, you stone-heads should thank me because I already have made the mistake of giving the worst answer possible for any question that involves state capitols," I calmly asserted as I was determined that nothing was going to bother me with my new found excited outlook on life.

"That's right!" announced Roger, "D.B. I remember when you told us that Jesse James had been President of Australia before the Civil War and before the United States got mad at Australia and kicked it out of the country by simply diggin' it up. I also remember when Oscar announced in class that California had fallen into the ocean around 1950 and scientists thought it was somewhere near the *Titanic*."

Between my ability to handle their insults, and Roger reminding them of their own mistakes, D.B. and Oscar decided to take their insulting act to someplace where they could get a "rise" out of someone. It was nice to see Roger back on my side and not trying to jab

151

me with petty jokes. I couldn't blame him for his teasing the day before, as I would have done the same thing to him.

"Do you know if you're go'un to the game or not?" asked Roger with hope.

"I'll be there. My Dad wants to see Chris' brothers play. I can't wait. I'll finally get to show Chris just how much she means to me. It will be our first unofficial official date," I said with a glow on my face that looked like I had just walked out of a nuclear reactor that was leaking radiation.

The rest of the week seemed to fly by. Nothing was going wrong. I felt on top of the world. For some reason the rest of the class gave up on teasing me as they could tell it wasn't bothering me and everything else seemed to fall in place. To top it all off, every time we left class I managed to get in line next to Chris and I even got to sit by her in art and lunch-what a great couple of days.

"See 'ya at the game tonight," I beamed as Chris and I were headed to the bus parking lot after school on Friday.

"I'm so glad you're coming. I can't wait until tonight," Chris added as we parted ways and got on our own buses.

Chapter 10

Bleacher Jumpin'

"What took ya so long?" bellowed Roger the instant he saw me walk through the doors next to the gym.

"Whadya mean?" I answered. "The game hasn't started yet has it?"

"No, but you gotta protect your woman. She's being held hostage by Carlos, D.B. and Oscar. All three of 'em are surroundin' her on the bleachers and they are really annoying her to death," informed the Twid in his I've got a plan voice.

About that time, my Dad put a heavy hand on my shoulder and pointed out where our family was going to sit. He also informed me to meet them just outside the gym doors after the game was over.

Now that I had the okay to sit wherever I wanted, I could focus my attention to helping Chris escape her tormentors. The only problem was that I couldn't sit next to her with my parents at the game. That would be a dead give away as to why I had to be at this particular game. It would also cause me grief since my parents would tell me things like-"You're too young to have a girlfriend," or "We now know the real reason why you wanted to go to the game." I simply couldn't afford to make them any more suspicious than they probably already were, but I still had to be able to spend quality time with Chris without my parents knowing it.

Roger decided to play Cupid once again without asking me. While I was pondering my situation, he took off to go tell Chris that I was there. I don't know exactly what he told her, but she elegantly excused herself from the midst of the henchmen and strode over to see me.

By now my heart was racing. I was a "bundle of nerves". I was glad to see Chris, but at the same time I was afraid my parents would see us and think something fishy was going on. I was also afraid that the henchmen would come over to hound us during the first break of action in the basketball game. Then, surely something would go wrong and embarrass both Chris and I. I knew, even if none of the above happened, Andie would probably show up at the most inopportune time, and create even more havoc in my life then she normally did.

Suddenly, my attention became diverted from Chris and my problems as I intently watched one of her brothers steal a pass from the opposing team and start racing up the right side of the court. At the same time, the other twin dashed up the left side of the court. When the twin with the ball reached the free throw line he tossed it toward the rim. As the ball neared the rim, the other twin grabbed it in mid flight and slammed it home. This awesome play brought the crowd to its feet followed by a deafening roar in approval of the great play.

I automatically turned to Chris to tell her, "Your brothers' are awesome!"

"They're not too bad," Chris agreed.

Shannon Gepford

"Not too bad," I started to retaliate when I noticed out of the corner of my eye how the crowd on the far side of the bleachers was still standing. Only, they were not facing the game. Everyone in that section was turned around and murmuring and pointing and gasping.

"What's going on over there?" I wondered aloud as I craned my neck to see between the people. "Scum-eatin' crap!" I shrieked as I realized what the crowd was staring at. It was my sister-Andie. She was stuck between the bleachers. Her upper torso was wedged between the seats, while her lower body was dangling in air. She was also panicked as she screamed and wiggled and cried, "HELP! Please!" The more she wiggled, the worse she became stuck.

By now, the whole gym knew what was going on. The referees stopped the game and sent each team to their bench as the high school principal grabbed the microphone and asked all the people in Andie's section and the surrounding sections to "Please get up and clear the bleachers." This was done so the bleachers on either side of Andie's section could be pushed in and someone could walk beneath where Andie was stuck to try to push or pull her out.

"What an idiot!" I remarked as I finally realized what a fine mess Andie had caused. No sooner than those words had left my mouth, I began counting my blessings for Andie's act of stupidity. I reasoned how I could make my "date" with Chris turn out the way I had hoped. I now knew that no one was paying attention to me so I could make my move.

I stealthily glided over to the concession stand and purchased a bag of peanut *M&M's* and a *Dr. Pepper.* As quickly as I had left, I reappeared by Chris' side and asked, "What did I miss?"

"Nothing," was Chris' reply, "Your sister is really stuck. They still can't get her out."

"Aw, she's not that fat. She otta' be able to squeeze outta there the same way she squeezed in," I mumbled with a mouthful of chocolate. "By the way, would you like a bite or a drink?"

Chris reached for the cup of pop as we both gazed in Andie's direction. My plan was now really working. I had paid for a pop and candy and I was sharing it with my gorgeous girlfriend. But, best of all, we were drinking out of the same cup and that was as good as kissing, since we were technically "swappin' spit."

Meanwhile, Andie was still stuck. No one could get her to budge. My dad was trying to pull her out from on top of the bleachers while another man was trying to pull her out from beneath. About the only thing that was working was Andie's lungs as she continued to wail louder and louder.

Finally an idea burst into my head. "Come on Chris! I gotta idea!" I blurted as I grabbed her hand and tossed away our pop cup all in one motion. I gently, but rapidly pulled Chris along behind me as we snaked our way through the crowd that was standing on the basketball court staring at my sister. As we snaked our way through the crowd, anytime we came in contact with a classmate I asked them to "Follow us."

After rounding up nine classmates—Oscar, D.B., Twid, Louis, Catherine, Carlos, Gretchen (who made two of Louis), Frank, and Sadie; I told them of my plan to get Andie unstuck. "We are all gonna stand on the bleacher row in front of where Andie is stuck," I announced.

"What good'll that do?" questioned Sadie.

"Plenty," I replied. "After standing in front of Andie, on the count of three we will all jump up and land on the bleacher. This will cause the boards to bow and give. As the boards bow, it will allow Andie an instant to be pulled out from beneath as the impact should be enough to get her unstuck for a split second."

"That won't work," harassed Carlos.

"Why not?" I questioned, "Do ya got a better idea?"

"Weell, for this to work," squeaked Louis, "we need my love kitten Gretchen to stand in front of Andie to give us the most leverage."

"Louis, what you mean is that we need Aunt Godzilla Gretchen to stand in front of Andie because she's the biggest and fattest of all of us," roared D.B.

"I'm gonna pound your skinny little weasel buns for that remark," bellowed Godzilla.

"Hey, I think Louis is onto something," interrupted Twid. "If the bigger kids are in the middle and the smaller kids like Louis are on the ends, it will make the bleachers bow more and be easier to get Andie out.

163

"Well what are we wait'un fer?" broke in Frank. "Christmas?"

At that moment all of us scampered to the bleacher and made our way up it until we were all facing Andie.

"Hey it's work'un!" blasted Carlos. "Look at how much the bleacher is bow'in underneath Godzilla now."

"I'm gonna..." trailed off Gretchen's voice as she was interrupted by Oscar's obnoxious laughter.

As my classmates traded insults with each other, I informed my Dad how we were going to get Andie free. I told him that he needed to be beneath Andie to both pull and catch her when the bow in the bleacher gave her that split second of freedom. I also informed him that the reason the adults couldn't do the bleacher jumping was because they were too heavy and if they jumped it might break the bleacher and create a bigger problem.

"Listen up!" spoke up my Dad, "When I count to three all of you kids jump up and land on the bleacher. Andie, at the instant they land, you will be jarred free and yanked down—so be prepared. Are we ready? One, two, three!"

At the instant my Dad hit "three" in his countdown all of us leaped high into the air and crashed down onto the bleacher seat with an emphatic stomping motion in hopes of giving the board a little extra bow in order to free Andie. Surprisingly, the plan worked. Andie was immediately jarred free. She came crashing down into my Father with a force that bowled him over. As they both lay on the gym floor beneath the bleacher, I saw a look of relief spread over Andie's face that was soon replaced by the look of fear that always precedes her "How much trouble am I going to get in?" thought. My Dad on the other hand, had a different, confused look that I hadn't seen before.

After surveying the situation and realizing that my family members were okay, I realized the rest of the crowd was cheering. What a neat feeling—they were actually cheering for my family and friends. I was starting to enjoy my time in the limelight; when, abruptly I was brought back into reality by Carlos.

"It's a wonder you didn't break the bleacher with that power leap Godzilla!" screamed Carlos.

"It's a wonder you had enough coordination to land on the bleacher after you jumped!" retaliated, Gretchen.

"Louis, I think I saw a little daylight under your feet," kidded Roger.

"Yeah, I could have leapt over a newspaper in a single bound," fired back Louis in an agreeing tone.

"Cool!" shrieked Frank.

"It actually worked," added Sadie in a tone of disbelief.

As I looked at the rest of my classmates, I could tell they were extremely proud of their act. D.B. and Oscar were giving each other both high and low fives, while Chris was grinning ear to ear. Admittedly, I was proud of myself for coming up with the idea.

Finally, after about ten more minutes, the game resumed. Funny thing though, the game seemed to be secondary to what was on everyone's mind the rest of the evening.

We did manage to win the game, but that is about all I can remember about it.

I did remember what happened before I left however. It was awesome and confusing all in the same moment. I had been holding Chris' hand since I had pulled her through the crowd. I hadn't realized that I had never let go of it through all the excitement. The moment I realized it so did my Dad. He slyly smiled and turned to walk out the gym door. As soon as he turned to go out the door, Chris reached over and gave me a kiss, on the lips, nonetheless. She did it so quickly, I didn't know what hit me until it was over. She also did it so quickly that only one person saw it— Roger.

"I love you," whispered Chris, "What you did for your sister proves I picked the right guy. I'll see you on Monday."

"Thank you," I stuttered, "I can't wait 'til Monday gets here."

At that point I was feeling on top of the world. I had gotten to pay for our food on our first date, I had gotten to hold Chris' hand (even if I hardly remembered it, but it had to be great). To top it all off, I had received my first kiss on the lips and been told I love you by the most gorgeous girl God had ever made. This string of events had made me feel like a king and that I could do no wrong. There was, however, one question that needed to be answered—I had to find out how and why Andie got stuck.

Shannon Gepford

My parents had pelted Andie with questions but they weren't getting anywhere. Finally they gave up and just chalked it up to one of those things that kids do that aren't the most intelligent things to do. I didn't buy it. I knew there was a reason for Andie getting stuck.

As we walked toward our car, my parents led the way while Andie and I followed behind out of earshot.

When I knew my parents couldn't hear me I whispered, "What's up. How and why did you get stuck?"

"I did it for you," she smiled.

"You did what!" I exclaimed as quietly as I could.

"Yes, I did it for you," Andie replied.

"That fall must have damaged your brain," I stated, "That is the most ridiculous thing that I have ever heard."

"Listen Sis, Roger asked me to create a distraction. He said that YOU needed some help tonight. I didn't know what he meant, but I had a good idea. I told him that I would do it on one condition. The condition was that he give me five bucks in advance and a kiss after it was over," spoke Andie as she pulled a crisp Abraham Lincoln out of her pocket.

I stood there in disbelief with my mouth hanging open when I saw Roger dart between the two cars nearest Andie and me. He motioned to Andie to hurry over. She quickly rushed over between the cars and in one motion they wrapped their arms around each other

171

and planted a kiss on each other's lips that would make liquid hydrogen melt.

Roger then said "Goodbye," to Andie, and "I love it when a plan comes together," to me, as he fled in the opposite direction before I could gather my composure to question him.

I tried to question and pry answers from Andie to no avail. She had done her job and was rewarded remarkably well in her own mind so she wasn't about to help me with the minor details. I finally gave up trying to get information from her. I eased my mind with the fact that even if Roger the Cupid was behind my good fortune with Chris, I didn't care because it had been the best evening of my life, and I could tell by looking at Andie that her evening hadn't been too shabby either.

About the Author

Writing about a boy growing up in rural Missouri was not hard for Shannon Gepford; he has lived his entire life in Bates County, which afforded him a great background for *Solomon Isaiah Spreewell*. He currently resides near Butler, Missouri, with his wife Misti and their two daughters, Alyx and Mady.

Shannon is a former teacher and coach and is the current Fellowship of Christian Athletes' sponsor for Adrian High School. He has written hundreds of weekly sports columns for *The Adrian Journal*, a rural newspaper. He has also had a poem— "Remember When" published in an anthology titled *Moments of Reflection* by The Poetry Guild in 1997. Shannon is currently working on another *Solomon Isaiah Spreewell* book.

Printed in the United States
776200002B